BORDER REPRISAL

BORDER REPRISAL

TIM CHAMPLIN

FIVE STAR

A part of Gale, Cengage Learning

GALE
CENGAGE Learning®

Farmington Hills, Mich • San Francisco • New York • Waterville, Maine
Meriden, Conn • Mason, Ohio • Chicago

LIBRARY OF CONGRESS CATALOGING-IN-PUBLICATION DATA

Names: Champlin, Tim.
Title: Border reprisal / by Tim Champlin.
Description: First edition. | Waterville, Maine : Five Star, a part of Gale, Cengage Learning, [2016]
Identifiers: LCCN 2015035865 | ISBN 9781432831578 (hardcover) | ISBN 1432831577 (hardcover) | ISBN 9781432831455 (ebook) | ISBN 1432831453 (ebook)
Subjects: LCSH: Gold theft—Fiction. | Outlaws—West (U.S.)—Fiction. | Train robberies—West (U.S.)—Fiction. | Mexican-American Border Region—Fiction. | GSAFD: Western stories.
Classification: LCC PS3553.H265 B67 2016 | DDC 813/.54—dc23
LC record available at http://lccn.loc.gov/2015035865

First Edition. First Printing: January 2016
Find us on Facebook– https://www.facebook.com/FiveStarCengage
Visit our website– http://www.gale.cengage.com/fivestar/
Contact Five Star™ Publishing at FiveStar@cengage.com

Printed in the United States of America
1 2 3 4 5 6 7 20 19 18 17 16

For my two youngest grandchildren,
Paul and Mary Champlin

CHAPTER 1

March 22nd, 1887
Southern Pacific Train
Mojave Desert

Wells Fargo express messenger Marc Charvein held his hands shoulder high and stared at the blue eyes behind a pair of holes cut in the bandit's flour sack hood. He tried to remain dead still, but the thumping in his chest seemed to shake his whole body. *Maybe he won't shoot while I'm holding his gaze,* Charvein thought. In the past, he'd felt the sharp bite and deep ache of bullets. He'd do everything in his power to keep from suffering that again.

Another damned robbery, and they caught us flat-footed. Charvein's disgust mingled with fear. He glanced out the open side door of the express car where the robber's mounted accomplice was holding the extra horse and smoking a cigar through the mouth hole in his hood.

The El Paso–bound Southern Pacific passenger train had been halted in the desert wilderness thirty miles west of Yuma.

"Open the safe!" The gunman jabbed his pistol barrel toward the iron safe next to the rolltop desk.

"Scared to show your faces, you damned vultures!" The voice came from Charvein's young assistant, Bob Billings.

Charvein shot him a warning glance.

"You could identify us, we'd have to kill you," the bandit replied matter-of-factly.

Charvein licked his dry lips, squatted by the safe, and began to work the combination.

"Yeah, that's it—give 'em everything they want." Billings' fair face was flushed.

"Shut up!" Charvein snapped.

In his haste, Charvein turned the dial too far past the second number. He wiped his sweaty palm on his pants and started over. *There!* He gripped the handle and turned. *Clunk!* The bolts slid back and the iron door swung open on silent hinges.

"Put it all in there." The hooded man tossed him a canvas sack.

Charvein shoved aside two tightly-wrapped packages to reach bound stacks of bank notes, bearer bonds, greenbacks, and several rolls of double eagles.

"I said, *all* of it!" the bandit snapped.

Charvein added the two heavy, canvas-bound packages to the loot and handed the sack back over his shoulder.

The bandit had to holster his gun to tie a loop in the slack top of the long sack.

Charvein stood up and took a step forward, but froze when the robber whipped out his revolver. The double click of the cocking hammer was loud in the silence.

A sudden vision of another episode flashed into his mind's eye. Years before, on a snowy mountainside in the Bitterroots, he'd startled a timber wolf at its kill of a jackrabbit. Charvein had frozen in place, rigid with sudden fear, the snarling wolf, only yards away. *Be calm and submissive,* he'd told himself. After several tense seconds with ears flattened and lips curling from white fangs, the rumbling in the throat subsided and the long, gray hunter snatched its prey and loped away into the dim spruce forest.

That same submissive reaction might save him now. He drew a slow breath and looked down, away from the black bore of the muzzle three feet from his face. This was no wild animal, but Charvein knew if he made any sudden moves, the nervous gunman would pull the trigger.

No amount of treasure was worth getting himself or Billings killed or wounded, Charvein reasoned. The robbers might win this round, but the fight was far from over. Yet, if he saw a crack in their armor and was quick enough . . .

"Don't move 'til we're outta sight." The man backed toward the open side door. His muffled voice sounded youthful. In Charvein's experience, young robbers were the most reckless—and dangerous.

Clutching the sack in one gloved fist and a revolver in the other, the robber turned and jumped down from the open side door of the express car and sprinted toward his mounted partner, who tossed him the reins of the extra horse.

As soon as the bandit turned his back, Charvein dove for his own pistol on the floor by the wall. In one continuous motion, he snatched it, rolled over, thrust the Merwin-Hulbert .32 at arm's length toward the open door, and snapped off two quick shots.

The mounted accomplice fired back, but his horse jumped and the slugs splintered a desk drawer just above Charvein's head.

One of Charvein's bullets found its mark, and the robber on foot howled and dropped his pistol. Still clutching the sack, he threw its loop over the saddle horn. The horse shied at the sudden roar of gunfire, walling its eyes and turning in a half-circle, dragging its reins, along with the man who was trying to mount. After two or three attempts, the cursing bandit gripped the saddle horn with his good left hand and vaulted into the saddle without using the stirrup. A red stain showed on his right shirtsleeve.

Charvein fired again and missed.

Wheeling their mounts, the two kicked them into a gallop. As they burst past the open side door, the hooded partner shouted something and hurled his smoking cigar into the car. Cigar? No—a burning fuse on a dynamite stick.

Reflexes launched Charvein into a two-foot space between the wall of the car and the big, iron safe. It was all that saved him. A thunderous roar smothered all sound, filling the space with smoke and flying pieces of wood and glass. The heavy safe was jolted back on big castors, pinning him against the wall. He held his breath against the acrid smoke burning his nose and eyes. Twisting, he managed to bring up one knee against the safe and pushed. The safe moved a few inches—enough so he could bend his other leg. Both knees gave him better leverage and, back against the wall, he shoved with all this strength. The big safe rolled two feet away, its castors crunching glass. Everything sounded dim.

He scrambled out of his snug prison, and looked around. The two bandits were gone and the smoke was dissipating, showing the bulging walls of the car at the other end and several square feet of the roof blown off, letting in the desert sun.

Bob Billings was on the floor. Charvein rushed to his assistant and turned him over. He was unconscious, bleeding from his nose and several small cuts.

"The end door's jammed." The conductor's head appeared at the open side door, followed by the engineer and fireman. "Is he dead?"

"No. Concussion must've knocked him out." Charvein felt gently for broken bones.

"Lemme see." The uniformed, gray-haired conductor vaulted up into the car. "You hurt, too?" he asked without looking at Charvein.

"I'm okay. The safe shielded me."

The conductor pulled out a pocket flask, uncapped it, and

held the silver container's metal neck under Billings' nose. The young man snorted, coughed, and opened his eyes, blinking a few times.

"Lie still a minute," the conductor said, pressing him back when he tried to rise. "Where're you hurting?"

Billings started to move his lean body. "Everywhere." He put a hand to his midsection. "Ribs and chest, mostly. Head hurts." He gingerly wiped the blood from his upper lip.

The engineer climbed into the wrecked car. "Undercarriage looks good. Guess she'll still roll. Won't have to uncouple." He turned and spat out his used-up chaw of tobacco, adding to the mess on the floor.

"Yeah." Charvein straightened up, his hearing slowly returning from a foggy distance. "Good thing it was just one stick of dynamite." He walked to the door and squinted out into the sun. "Bastards got what they came for. Don't know why they had to wreck the car, too."

"Yeah, you gave 'em everything without a fight," Billings said, being helped to a sitting position by the conductor.

Charvein looked back at him without replying. He knew the 20-year old was bitterly disappointed at being passed over for promotion three months earlier. Wells Fargo District Superintendent Barton Coughlin had instead hired the older, more experienced Marc Charvein to fill the job of lead express messenger on the run between Los Angeles and El Paso. Youthful resentment was one thing Charvein didn't want to deal with at the moment. Let the kid think what he wanted. He'd realize later that Charvein had made the right decisions.

He braced a hand on the floor and jumped down outside to see if the wounded bandit might have dropped any of the money. Apparently, the neck of the sack was tied securely enough to keep all its contents.

The midday sun glinted on metal. He crouched and picked

up the outlaw's revolver apparently dropped when Charvein's bullet struck his arm. It wasn't the common Colt. The shiny bluing was nearly new. He squinted at the barrel stampings—a British-made Webley-Pryse from the London Armoury. It was a top-break revolver very similar to one he'd seen in Gunterson's Virginia City gun shop last year when he'd bought his own Merwin-Hulbert. He pressed the lever behind the cylinder and released the catch. Barrel and cylinder tilted forward and the star ejector automatically pushed out all six unfired cartridges. The base of each shiny brass shell was stamped *.45 Cal.* He dropped the six cartridges into his vest pocket and snapped the revolver closed. He hefted it. The nicely shaped, sloping grip of checkered walnut fit his hand perfectly. A double action, the weapon had a five-inch octagonal barrel and weighed maybe two pounds. He pulled the trigger to test its action. Smooth. Drawing his own Merwin-Hulbert, he shoved the Webley into its place. *Mister Webley-Pryse, you're entirely too nice a revolver for a bandit. I'm adopting you.* He stuck his smaller .32 under his belt.

His boots crunched gravel ballast forty yards past the caboose. Then he stopped and gazed at the slurred hoofprints winding between two sand dunes and disappearing toward the southwest. The robbers couldn't have left an easier trail to follow—easy, that is, until a few hours of incessant desert wind erased the tracks as if they'd never existed. Doubtless the trail would continue south across the Mexican border only a few miles away; there was nowhere closer in this desert waste to hide. What lay on the other side of the line was a mystery to him. More of the same, he guessed.

After several similar holdups in the past few months, a reporter for the *Los Angeles Daily Times* had dubbed the anonymous robbers the Border Brigands. The name had stuck and been taken up by other papers, including the *Arizona Sentinel.*

Charvein bit his lip and pondered his first encounter with the Border Brigands. This made the seventh robbery since October, the first since Charvein had come aboard as head express messenger on this run between the coast and west Texas. Wells Fargo had hired him to protect the company shipments, but he'd failed his first test. Not a good omen for long employment. Maybe Bob Billings was right—he'd given in too easily. But the kid would likely have gotten himself killed resisting the robbery. There was more than one way to skin a bandit, he thought, turning back toward the shattered express car. He had his work cut out for him. They'd notify the U.S. Marshal's office at Yuma within the hour, of course. But neither the local sheriff nor U.S. territorial law enforcement agents had any authority across the border in Mexico. He suspected there was a lot more to these holdups than just random robberies. He'd been a railroad detective in the past. But this time he'd been hired to protect and defend the shipments, not to hunt down the bandits. Yet, he itched to research the details of the other recent holdups to see if he could detect a pattern.

He walked back alongside the train, circling a half-dozen men who'd alighted from the two passenger coaches and were conversing in low tones among themselves. He wore no uniform, and if they knew he was the express car messenger, they didn't let on, only stared at him curiously as he passed. Apparently, it was the look on his face that averted any questions. They must've heard the explosion and could see the damaged car for themselves.

"We need to make up a little time." The lean engine driver was mopping his face with a red bandanna when Charvein strolled up. "But I'll have to take it a bit easier until I see how that weakened car rolls."

The fireman and brakeman were wielding shovels to clear the track of a four-foot pile of sand.

"Effective way of stopping a train in a treeless desert," Charvein remarked, then wished he'd kept silent.

"Hell, I *had* to stop." The engineer sounded defensive. "Couldn't plow through it. We'd have been derailed."

"Yeah, glad you were alert." Charvein nodded his approval, thinking how the panic stop had thrown him and Billings out of their chairs to the floor, and generally scrambled the contents of the express car. "All that sand looks alike from a distance. Hard to see."

The conductor, who'd been attending the injured Billings, jumped down from the express car. "Okay, everybody back aboard," he yelled, waving his arm. "We're getting underway."

The passengers flipped away their cigars and climbed up the steps.

Like some great beast, the compact 4-6-0 mogul locomotive stood panting softly, awaiting the order to move, curved black sides glistening with condensed steam.

Charvein headed for the express car. The robbers had slithered out of the desert like two sidewinders, struck with poisoned fangs, then disappeared with their prey. It reminded him of tales he'd read about bandits armed with scimitars attacking camel trains in the Sahara. But, unlike those in North Africa, these raiders had killed no one—so far.

He gritted his teeth in frustration. Facing his boss with this would not be pleasant.

CHAPTER 2

"You wanted to see me, sir?" Marc Charvein tried to look calm and professional when he entered the office of the Wells Fargo district superintendent.

"Yes. Close the door." Barton Coughlin glanced up from his desk. The fact that he wanted the door shut in spite of the heat gave Charvein a clue as to the man's mood. The weather in late March in Yuma was like early June in any normal climate. Coughlin had shed his coat, but retained the tie with the starched white shirt and stiff collar.

Ill at ease, Charvein stood in the middle of the small office, waiting for the boss to finish whatever he was writing. The superintendent hadn't addressed him by name—even if he remembered it—had not risen from his desk to greet him, had made no eye contact, had not offered him a chair.

Barton Coughlin, Charvein knew from company rumors, was a man whose job was in jeopardy from his superiors because of this string of robberies.

Finally, the boss returned the steel-nibbed pen to its holder and looked up. "I suppose you know why I called you here."

The games had begun. God, how Charvein hated bureaucratic officiousness! Why couldn't people just talk man-to-man like adults? "Not really," he replied. "I sent my written report over from the hotel by courier."

"I saw it." He paused and smoothed his drooping mustache that completely hid his mouth.

I suppose this is how men earn their pensions, Charvein thought. *He's been ordered to crack down on me, as the newest employee.*

Coughlin was within four years of retirement. He'd started out with Wells Fargo in the San Francisco office during the 1850 gold rush days and had risen through the ranks, willing to take any transfer and do any job to get ahead. The district superintendent was probably as high as he could go, but he was still in danger of being terminated before he could collect his pension.

"When you came aboard with the company, I thought I made it very clear what we'd been faced with since last fall. It was my hope and plan that you'd help us put a stop to it."

"Yessir." This required nothing but agreement.

"Tell me in your own words what happened."

Charvein repeated what he'd written in his report, elaborating on a few details. ". . . and the rest you know," he finished. He didn't mention confiscating the pistol the wounded robber had dropped. The bandit had been wearing doeskin gloves so there was no chance an identification could be attempted by the newly developing science of fingerprinting.

Coughlin sat back in his desk chair, stroking a smoothly shaved chin. His face had a rosy tint, offset by pasty-looking bags under his eyes. The thinning dark hair was combed over on top, and Charvein found himself wondering what Coughlin would have looked like as a new employee thirty-five years ago. Probably slim, dark-haired, with curly, mutton-chop sideburns—a young man eager to please—a company man all the way. No hint of a rebellious nature, or any independent thinking. A man didn't rise to this position by bucking the system or needling his bosses.

Charvein waited as the silence stretched out to painful length. He wished the old man would open a window to admit some air.

"What will you do to prevent another violent robbery?" Coughlin finally asked, throwing the ball to him, even though he felt sure Coughlin already had a plan.

Charvein was prepared. "Well, sir, all the attacks have occurred in daylight. Should they continue into the heat of summer, I expect the brigands'll switch tactics and use the cooler cover of darkness . . ."

"Continue? Dammit, man!" His open palm smacked the desktop with a crack like a gunshot.

Charvein started.

"We can't *allow* them to continue. We must stop them—*now.* One more attempt must be their last!" His pink complexion suffused to red. The stiff celluloid collar appeared to be choking him.

"Yessir!"

Coughlin was apparently under more tension than the mainspring of a cocked Colt .45. "The company is losing money—a lot of money. In order for Wells Fargo to compete with the United States Post Office for business, we insure every parcel in our care. That means we reimburse full value for any losses that occur while a customer's valuable parcels are in our possession."

Charvein nodded. He was well aware of the policy. "Mister Coughlin, I have a couple of ideas I'd like to try, but don't have all the details worked out yet. Do I have a free hand to try something different? It won't involve asking for outside help," he added, sensing Coughlin would be made to look inept if he didn't solve the problem internally.

The superintendent's eyelids narrowed to slits above the pouches of flesh. "Within reason. But I must give final approval before you implement anything."

"Fair enough." He began to relax a little, though he was still standing in front of the boss's desk. "I've had experience as a

17

railroad detective," he continued in a professional tone. "In order to get a better idea of what we're dealing with, may I look at the reports on the previous robberies?"

Coughlin nodded. "I have them right here, and you can study them in the outer office. They must not leave this building." He pulled open a side desk drawer and drew out several manila folders. "When you're done, leave them with my clerk out front and he'll return them to the safe."

"Anything else, sir?" Charvein stepped forward and scooped up the pile of folders.

"Yes." He motioned for Charvein to hand back the files. Coughlin flipped open the top folder and removed several sheets of paper. "Okay, take them."

What was so confidential that the lead express messenger couldn't see it? He guessed it was probably Bob Billings' written comments blasting Charvein's alleged cowardice. "When's my next run?" he inquired aloud.

"Tomorrow afternoon. You'll relieve the man from El Paso for the return to the coast."

"Is Billings all right, sir?" Charvein had earlier resolved not to bring up the name of his feisty co-worker, but felt he needed to. "He took quite a jolt from that dynamite blast."

Coughlin again narrowed his eyes and studied him before replying. "Yeah, he's okay. As you know, I sent him on to finish the run to El Paso after we shunted the damaged car to the yards."

"Tough youngster," Charvein commented, to get in a last word in his own defense. "He'll make a good express messenger—if he lives long enough." He reached for the door handle.

CHAPTER 3

Sonoran Desert
Arizona Territory

Carlos Sandoval stood up from his tiny campfire of dry mesquite twigs and stretched tired muscles in his back and shoulders. The familiar fatigue and soreness would make him sleep well tonight.

A slight stirring of air from the cooling land fanned his face as he stared at a blend of red and gold cirrus clouds above the horizon. Since he was likely the only human for miles, he considered it a spectacle put on for his benefit. Every evening it was the same, yet ever-changing, and he never tired of watching the brilliant colors mixing, morphing, sliding down the blue canvas of sky to gradually fade into night. He knew what caused the spectacular show, and it wasn't magic. But he smiled to himself, recalling a quote attributed to humorist, Mark Twain, when speaking of a savage who didn't understand the making of a rainbow vs. a civilized man who did—"We've lost as much as we gained by prying into that matter."

Through the previous mild winter months, Sandoval had followed a similar routine—riding his mule, Jeremiah, and leading his pack burro, Lupida, on a quest for rich color across miles of cactus-studded Sonoran Desert. He ranged between the Castle Dome mining district and the Colorado River. Habitually, he spent long hours trudging in and out of rocky arroyos, scaling nearly inaccessible ledges to chip off promising ore samples, collecting tiny nuggets and flakes of gold from streambeds after flash floods. Later they'd be smelted by an assayer in Yuma and traded for necessary staples at some general store. He had no burning desire to strike it rich, and was content to find enough trace metal to subsist. Striking enough good ore for a mine meant trouble, work, and worry. Wealth brought ease, but also conflict with other humans who would take what you had, legally, or illegally.

He admitted to himself his present drifting existence was pointless. But for now he was content to apply the soothing balm of nature to his past injuries before taking up the conflict with others of his kind. His mule and burro were all the living company he needed while he crisscrossed the desert wastes a few miles from the unmarked boundaries of active, working mines. Each day's travel brought him a short way east or west, trending always north from Yuma. Yet, he was mindful he couldn't stray into the arid interior or wander too far or too long from some source of water. Now, his leather water bags lay nearly flat on the ground nearby, and he planned to end the next day's trek at the Colorado River several miles west.

For ten more minutes, he gazed at the western sky suffused with red and gold of the vanished sun. It was now late March and nights weren't nearly as frigid as they'd been three months ago, but his heat-thinned blood still needed a blanket after dark. As a loner with no partner to share guard duty, he made a habit of picketing his mule and burro fifty yards from where he bedded down, relying on the animals to sound the alarm if anyone—cougar, javelina, or human—approached. Burros were especially good at using their sharp hooves on rattlers.

Sandoval had spent most of the previous five years living a solitary life—the first four years as a fugitive with his animals in Lodestar, a Nevada ghost town. Much of the last few months, he'd been a prospector in the western Arizona Territory, only interrupting his routine for a wild, dangerous adventure with his old friend from Lodestar, Marc Charvein.

As twilight came on, he felt a slight chill between his shoulder blades—a chill he couldn't attribute to the cooling of his sweaty body. For the past three days, he'd experienced the sensation of being stalked. Yet, he'd seen no one—neither human nor animal. Maybe he was just becoming jumpy from being alone so long. But he couldn't shake the feeling, and he'd come to trust his instincts.

He reached for the binoculars that lay on a pack nearby. Their twin lenses concentrated much of the fading light and brought middle distances into focus. He swept them around at the undulating desert landscape—low and flat to the west and south, a gentle upslope to the north with a steeper incline to the east. He saw movement. From this distance, it resembled a kit fox, but he couldn't be sure. Century plants, mesquite, and ocotillo stood out in sharp relief in the fading light and clear air. No threat of danger anywhere that he could detect.

He swung down the glasses by their strap to the pack on the ground and crouched to see if the coffee water was boiling over the small fire.

Boom!

The coffeepot exploded six inches from his hand, spraying his shirtsleeve with scalding water. He fell back, scrambling to reach a dry wash a few yards away. He was rolling into it when a second shot kicked up dirt two feet behind him. Panting, he yanked his long-barreled Colt and squinted at the low hill two-hundred fifty yards to the east that provided the only cover anywhere around. The shot had come from that direction. His own body must have been silhouetted against the brightness of the western sky, making a clear target. A man shooting downhill from that distance tended to fire high, so it had been a very good shot, missing him by only a few inches. The mangled coffeepot lay on its side in the ashes, steam still rising from the fire.

The binoculars were barely within reach. He dragged them to him, adjusted the focus, and scanned the hill. A tendril of white smoke drifted up and away on the whisper of breeze.

Sandoval remained motionless, his heart rate beginning to slow as he studied the terrain for any sign of the shooter. Whoever had fired was using a big bore rifle, and was out of range of his pistol, an 1862 model open-top Colt percussion that had been converted to fire cartridges. The smoke told him where the shooter was, or had been. But the amount of smoke was slight. If the bushwhacker had been using the new smokeless powder cartridges, there likely would have been nothing at all to see. Did the shooter have a telescopic sight, or the old, flip-up adjustable Vernier sight?

Yet the major questions were: who and why? Carefully keeping his head below the lip of the wash, he twisted around to find his animals. Jeremiah and Lupida were still forty yards downslope from him, staring in his direction, apparently startled by the gunfire. At least they were at too low an angle to be seen from the eastern hill.

Whoever had tried to kill him might not give up now, even though Sandoval was alerted by the near miss. Coming darkness would provide cover if the shooter tried to creep up on the camp. But, would a bushwhacker have that much courage? Or would he wait and try again later from long range when he had all the advantage?

Sandoval could think of no enemies he had. Perhaps this was just some lone bandit who was attacking him for his ore samples, guns, or animals. Surely, there were more promising victims than a solitary, ragged prospector. It could be some renegade Apache coming down on a lone white man. Bronco Apaches frequently jumped the reservation at San Carlos and went raiding. But usually they traveled in groups of two or more. Maybe there was more than one man out there. No, if that were the case, they would have come right up close and attacked him, relying on surprise and numbers. A single Apache with a rifle, on the other hand, would take no chances. Fearless fighters all, Apaches males were still taught to take whatever advantage they could.

A niggling doubt troubled him about that theory—every Indian he'd ever encountered was a poor shot, with both long gun and pistol. Whoever this was had made a very good shot from long distance, shooting downhill in uncertain light.

In the dimness he examined his stinging forearm where the water had scalded him. A darker mark showed on his reddish brown skin. Nothing serious. He'd rub some bacon grease on it.

What now? Wait for cover of darkness, then salvage what he could of his gear and slip away to the west and make for the Colorado River about seven miles to the west? The shooter might anticipate his escape and circle around to head him off. In this open desert with a gibbous moon, he and the animals would be visible enough to a rifleman. Sandoval would have to move quickly between full dark and moonrise. Since he was part Indian himself, stealth was second nature. His own Marlin carbine was loaded and ready in a saddle sheath on the ground near his riding mule.

Minute followed minute and no more shots came. The shooter could obviously see the camp. But he wouldn't see anything for long as dusk was pulling a black blanket over the desert.

Sandoval had never lacked patience, and he didn't panic. He'd been in tight places before, and would do what needed to be done. He took off his wide straw hat, set it on the long barrel of his Colt, and slid it up above the lip of the arroyo. It drew no fire. The shooter had either moved to another vantage point, was waiting for a better shot, or had withdrawn.

Whatever, the case, Sandoval would be prepared to slip away when dusk faded to full dark. The campfire was now visible as only a few red embers that had escaped the dousing coffee water.

He forced himself to wait another fifteen minutes before he crept noiselessly downslope, retrieved his saddle blanket, and saddled his mule.

Then, as quietly as possible, he felt around and gathered his few utensils, sliding them into a pack, cringing when metal clanked on metal. But he guessed the shooter would wait for a better opportunity than shooting blindly at a noise. He cinched the packsaddle on the burro, then lashed the packs atop it, including the nearly empty leather water bags. Overall, a light load for the sturdy burro.

He removed the hobbles, and step by careful step, led the animals away from camp, heading west, scraping past mesquite bushes, stumbling into barrel cactus and rocks, being jabbed by Spanish bayonet. When he estimated they'd gone a quarter mile, he mounted the mule, took up the lead rope, and proceeded at a cautious walk, conscious that even the sure-footed mule could step into an unseen burrow and ruin a leg. In the dark, he had no sense of progress made, but knew by the stars they were moving west toward the river.

It seemed no time at all before the landscape began to lighten with the rising of the moon. He unsheathed his Marlin and laid it across the saddle horn.

Chapter 4

Marcus Aurelius Vance, M.D., contract surgeon for the U.S. Army, had just completed an exhausting three-day trip to and from Fort Huachuca, Arizona Territory. M.A. Vance, as he was generally known, groaned from the pain of his rheumatism as he stepped down stiffly from his buggy. *Maybe I should've accepted Colonel Fitzhugh's invitation to stay the night,* he thought. But he'd had all the human company he needed for a time. After treating guardhouse prisoners for various contusions they'd suffered in a saloon fight, resetting the badly broken leg of a trooper whose horse fell before the rider could jump clear, and dosing numerous digestive ailments and social diseases, and one case of snake bite, Vance didn't feel up to making small talk and jokes with several officers over supper in the commandant's quarters. He'd made his excuses and Fitzhugh had delegated a soldier to harness Vance's horse for the return trip to the lonely adobe house the doctor called home forty miles southwest of the fort.

Vance paused for a long, still minute, holding his horse by the dangling reins and looked out where the sweeping desert valley was streaked by long shadows cast by the declining sun. Perfect silence as nature balanced between day and night. The view was the reason he'd chosen this place to live, ignoring the military's mandate of living on the post where he was assigned. But the government was too short of doctors to enforce the rule. Between two massive mountains, the broad valley sloped southward for several miles. The Mexican border was out there somewhere, unmarked and undefined. Streaks of green marked two small streams. The landscape was covered by many varieties of desert shrubs. Dusk was creeping slowly over the valley floor.

In spite of its wild beauty, this remote location was one his wife, Constance, was never easy about. She complained the mountains and far distances were so huge they overwhelmed and dwarfed all humans. She felt like a tiny insect by comparison to the vast landscape. She complained of other things as well—his frequent trips to the military posts in the southern part of the territory. He offered to take her along, but after two bone-jarring trips over the rutted trails that passed for roads, she decided to stay home.

They'd not been blessed with children, and had passed into middle age moving from one rude military post to another until they'd settled in this abandoned adobe he had repaired for "their last house at the ends of the earth" as she put it. Fearful of her surroundings, but with nowhere to go but an occasional shopping trip to Tucson, she became morose. During a chilly, damp January, three months earlier, she'd contracted pneumonia. In spite of his best efforts to treat her, she weakened rapidly and died within a week. Dead at sixty-one. After her fear of nocturnal pumas, of the desert diamondbacks, herds of javelinas, tarantulas, and scorpions, of hard outlaws and rustlers who sometimes used this valley to escape south across the border—and especially her dread of rumored Apache torture, it was actually a silent killer from within that took her.

Vance began to unharness the patient Morgan, thinking Constance might still be alive if she hadn't lost her will to live. In his years of medical practice, Vance had seen the mind triumph over great odds before. But, from his observation, she'd given up. He knew it was probably his own fault because he'd refused to live in the rough quarters furnished by the military on the various frontier posts. At least there she would've had the company of other women—officers' wives, mainly. Cooking, sharing recipes, babysitting with small children, watching mounted drills, hearing the sergeants' shouted commands, thrilling to rumors of Apache uprisings, regulating one's day by calls of the bugler—all these things and other distractions might have kept the flame of life burning longer for Constance.

He sighed. Too late now. If one couldn't correct his mistakes, he had to live with them. He had two consoling thoughts: the majority of their married life had been happy, especially the early years, when everything was a new adventure. Secondly, his wife of thirty-seven years was now beyond the reach of any earthly worry or pain.

Scooping some oats into the feed box, he turned the Morgan into the attached stable, then grabbed his black bag and short, double-barreled coach gun out of the buggy and entered the house. The homemade latch would not have kept out any intruder; it was only designed to keep the door from blowing open.

In the gloom, he struck a match to a coal oil lamp, and turned up the wick. The soft, yellow glow dispersed shadows into the corners.

A quick supper of tortillas and beans would hold him for now. He lifted one of the iron stove-lids and shoved in splinters of wood and shavings. A match set it ablaze.

While the fire caught and flared up, he unhooked and threw open the green shutters, leaned on the windowsill, and stared out at the gathering dusk. A gentle breeze fanned through the glassless opening and he breathed in the aroma of desert sage.

His thoughts turned once again to resigning from the Army. He was sixty-six years old and had been at this long enough. Time to return to some civilized part of the country and take it easy. If he was careful, the money he'd saved would satisfy his simple needs. He could relocate near family. There were a few cousins and nephews in southern Illinois. But, even as these random thoughts crossed his mind, he knew it was a bad idea. He hadn't seen them in years and was no longer part of their lives. He barely knew the younger generation at all. Boredom would pounce on him quicker than lonely old age or poverty.

He heated up the beans and ate them with onions on a tortilla, slaking his thirst with a tin cup of hard cider. Almost time to restock his supplies, he thought as he finished and washed his plate with water from a tiny spring that bubbled up in a stone basin at a far corner of the room. The unknown builder of this place had located wisely. Vance wondered if the man had fallen to Apaches who were jealous of scarce watering holes.

Medicine provided Vance's livelihood; literature supplied his spiritual nourishment. He'd accumulated a couple of shelves of books—mostly classics—which had borne more than one reading. Fiction and nonfiction furnished him an escape. This trip he'd borrowed from the Fort Huachuca library a copy of the recently published, *Life on the Mississippi.* He sat down in his ratty armchair and positioned the lamp to one side. He could hardly wait to dip into the thick volume. Twain was always entertaining.

But, he'd underestimated the depth of his weariness. The trip, the food, the hard cider all combined to weigh him down. He put a finger between the pages of the book and leaned his head back to rest his eyes for a minute . . .

Bang! Bang!

He jerked awake. The book slid off his lap, thudding to the stone floor.

Another tattoo rattled the plank door.

"Who is it?" He reached for the loaded shotgun leaning against the wall, eared back both hammers, and stepped to one side of the door.

"Doctor Vance," came a muffled voice. "Diego Sanchez from San Felipe. Come quick."

He exhaled in relief. The name was familiar—the blacksmith's apprentice from the village across the border. These poor people had called on him several times since discovering his presence in this lonely canyon. Vance's heart had been touched by their poverty and he always helped, stoutly refusing any payment of a chicken or vegetables.

"Entre," he replied. "The door is open."

He didn't lower the shotgun until the door was thrust back and two dark faces appeared in the lamplight. The taller youth was, indeed, Diego and Vance didn't recognize the slender, smaller one, whom, he suspected, was probably fleeter of foot. "What brings you out of your *casas* when the ghosts of Apaches walk in the moonlight?" he asked, lowering the hammers on the gun.

"Mi padre es . . ."

"Speak English." Vance interrupted the smaller of the two.

"His father has been shot by *bandidos,*" Diego replied.

"Where was he hit?"

"Here." The older boy put a hand to his side, which could mean anything.

"How many times?"

"Once."

"Is the bullet still in him?"

Diego and the younger boy conversed rapidly in Spanish.

"Sí."

"When did this happen?"

"Miércoles."

"Wednesday. Two days ago. Does he have fever?"

"Sí."

"Let me get my bag and we'll go. Did you boys run and walk

all the way from the village?"

"*Sí.*"

It was at least four miles. He knew they were hardened to such exertion and would have thought nothing of it. They'd probably started at dark to keep from being spotted by any Apaches or bandits.

Within a few minutes the Morgan was hitched and the three of them were in the buggy.

Vance popped the reins over the Morgan's back and guided him down the darkened trail. The bright moon would light the faint track. If Vance wandered off, the horse or the boys would let him know it.

"Did *bandidos* raid San Felipe?" he asked, clucking to the horse. It seemed inconceivable that any robbers would attack the villagers who were as dirt poor as any humans Vance had ever seen.

"*Sí.* They came to rob his *padre*—Juan Fortuna." Diego pointed at the younger boy. "When Señor Fortuna would not give them what they wanted, they shot him and tore up the house."

What could they have been looking for? "Was your mother harmed?" He directed his question at the smaller boy.

"No," Diego answered for him. "Only frightened."

"Did these Mexican *bandidos* come by night?" Vance asked.

"When the noon Angelus was ringing," Diego said.

So the wound was about two and a half days old, and probably mortified, if the patient was running a fever.

"Let us hurry and see if we can help." Vance slapped the reins over his tired Morgan. The horse broke into a trot on a long downgrade in the bright moonlight.

The April night had cooled off rapidly by the time the trio reached the village. But a stuffy, fetid odor assaulted Doctor

Vance's nose when the boys ushered him into the adobe hut of Juan Fortuna. The doctor paused inside the door, black bag in hand, allowing his eyes to adjust to the light of half a dozen candles burning by the head of the pallet where a man lay. A woman sat on the floor by his side.

During his moment of hesitation, Vance wondered if this family couldn't afford coal oil for a lamp, or if these were blessed religious candles burning. Vance had visited San Felipe before, but never this house. Diego said something to the woman, who stood up, nodded to Vance, and moved to one side so the doctor could examine the patient he took to be her husband. The candlelight reflected in her eyes, which were bright with tears. Her graying hair was pulled back from her lined face. Though he guessed her age to be on the shy side of forty, she looked every bit of fifty.

"Diego, bring in my shotgun," Vance said, quietly. The chances were slim that any outlaws would return this night, but he didn't want to be completely helpless if they did.

The boy was back in a minute and placed the shotgun on the dirt floor near Vance. "I'll give your horse a rubdown and some hay," Diego said.

"*Gracias.*"

Juan Fortuna was semi-conscious and sweating profusely. His wife came close and wiped her husband's face with a damp cloth. A scattering of damp black hair curled on his chest.

Vance snipped the crudely wrapped cotton bandage, lifted it with his scissors, and sniffed infection. He wished the boys had called him earlier. He motioned for the son to help slide his father's pallet just outside the open door into the cool, cleaner air.

Juan moaned.

The doctor supported the wounded man's head with one arm. "Juan, wake up! Swallow this."

The patient roused just enough to gulp water from a tin cup and wash down the quinine tablets. Then Vance went to work on the wound, probing for the bullet he suspected was only an inch or so below the surface. The good news was the bullet might not have hit anything vital. Being as gentle as he could, he probed for the lead slug, pausing when the patient cried out. Finally he found and extracted it, dropping it on the ground. Next, lacking any sterile water, he washed the wound with carbolic acid, then cleaned away as much of the infected flesh around it as he could.

Diego returned and stood back to watch.

"Ask the woman if she'll boil some water to clean this wound," he told the boy.

An hour later, Vance had done all he could and Juan Fortuna was drifting in and out of consciousness. "We must pray the infection does not kill him." Vance rose and returned instruments and gauze to his bag.

"He has been shot before," Diego said. "He is strong."

"That doesn't mean he will survive this," Vance said. "Ask his wife if the *bandidos* were after something special. Did they attack anyone else in the village?"

Diego translated. The careworn woman replied in rapid Spanish with many gestures.

"She said no one else was attacked. She said they kept demanding gold. As you can see, they are very poor."

"Odd," Vance muttered to himself, buckling the straps on his leather bag. "Maybe they had him mixed up with someone else." He turned to Diego. "Here, you boys help me take him back inside." Willing hands gripped the edge of the pallet.

"What is his wife's name?" Vance asked when the patient was again resting under shelter.

"Consuela."

"Tell her I'll sleep in my buggy and check on him when daylight comes in a few hours."

Diego translated. She turned to Vance and said something in Spanish. The only word he recognized was *"gracias."*

He waved off her thanks but she reached into the pocket of her faded apron and brought out a coin, handing it to him. He started to refuse, then saw it glint softly. Surprised, he took it and held it close to the flickering light of a candle. It was a disc of gold about the size of a fifty-dollar gold piece. But this was like nothing he'd ever seen. It had the rather crude look of something hand forged. One side was stamped with a simple cross and the other with an arrow. There was no date or other inscription. A one-of-a-kind family heirloom handed down from some Spanish ancestor? He doubted it. These Fortunas would have long since been forced to spend it for sustenance to stay alive. Besides, the gold disc, or coin of exchange if that's what it was, appeared new. There was no discernible wear to the surface or the sharp edges. Apparently, a hand-minted gold piece.

Diego was watching him. "Where did this come from?" Vance asked. "It could be the reason this man was shot."

"Quien sabe." Diego shrugged without bending down for a closer look, which told Vance the boy had seen it or one like it before. Vance didn't want to appear greedy, but had to know if others of its kind existed in the village.

"If this coin has brothers and sisters, I will keep it for now." Vance hoped Diego would tell him more. But Diego, slim apprentice to the town's blacksmith, wore an inscrutable face in the light of the candles that flickered by the light of the unconscious Juan Fortuna. The boy said nothing.

Chapter 5

Carlos Sandoval sensed his pursuer could be drawing a bead on him at any moment. The rising moon silvered the desert landscape, giving potential human shape to the arms of distant saguaro cactus, hiding potential snipers in the mesquite, yucca, or creosote bush.

Riding his mule and leading his pack burro, Sandoval knew he made an inviting silhouette for anyone watching with a rifle. He had no idea if the man was within rifle range, was still stalking him, or possibly had even given up the pursuit. Every few seconds he twisted in the saddle to search for any sign of the sniper who'd tried to bushwhack him in camp at sundown.

If only he had some inkling of who or why anyone would attack him, it might help him figure out a way to escape. As it was, he felt helpless.

He held his Marlin across the pommel to be ready if his attacker was somewhere out there, patient and persistent. Yet he knew, even in the uncertain light, there was a better than even chance a bullet could take him before he could even raise his carbine.

As the moon rose higher in the clear sky, Sandoval grew so uneasy he shoved the Marlin back into the saddle sheath and dismounted. He would lead his mule to make himself less visible for any watcher.

The mesquite bushes were evenly spaced as if someone had planted them—nature's way of spacing the plants so each could have sufficient moisture. But his progress was slowed by the prickly pear, Spanish bayonet, and cholla. He caught his breath as a yucca thorn stabbed his thigh. He moved carefully away from the cactus, even as he knew the spines and thorns were raking the sides and legs of his animals as well.

He tried to anticipate what his stalker might do. There were no hills within a mile or more to use for cover. He estimated the Colorado River was another six or seven miles to the west. His attacker wouldn't know that Sandoval was nearly out of water.

Twenty minutes later he halted the animals, uncased his field glasses, and scanned the surrounding terrain. Nothing unusual. He made another slow circle with the glasses. There! Movement! Two-hundred yards away something crossed an open patch of ground. He finely tuned the focus. There it was again. He looked intently. Then he slowly lowered the glasses and let out a long sigh. It was only a small herd of six or seven foraging javelinas. Maybe he was on edge for no reason. Perhaps the shooter of several hours earlier was just a passing outlaw, eager to try out the accuracy of a new rifle by having a little fun and blasting a coffeepot out of Sandoval's hands. There were people who thought a near-miss shot like that to scare some stranger half to death would be great entertainment.

Even as this thought passed through his mind, he knew he couldn't rely on such an assumption. He had to act as if the shooter was deadly serious.

He leaned against the saddle and rested his head on his forearm. After the sudden scare and letdown of seeing the wild pigs, the adrenaline was ebbing and he was sagging badly. This wouldn't do. He estimated it was still an hour until midnight. He'd been up and going since daylight, tramping in the hot sun all day with only a bite of cold bacon and a piece of dry bread in eighteen hours. His body cried for rest. But he had to push on until he reached the Colorado shortly before dawn. If he wasn't attacked before that, he could fort up with the river at his back, have plenty of water, and be ready for whatever came. *Focus on the river.*

He took up the reins and started again, leading the mule, Jeremiah, and the burro, Lupida, trailing after. The moonlight showed the spiny cactus and mesquite bushes as dark clumps, enabling him to navigate among them. Time became meaningless; the moon seemed pasted to the black sky. Machine-like, he plodded along, one foot ahead of the other, his mind a blank, the patient animals following.

By moonset, he estimated they'd trudged five more miles. He had to be getting close. The desert vegetation was thinning out. Thank God for open spaces and returning darkness. Traveling would be easier now. He was nearly numb and didn't want to interrupt his rhythm to stop and rest, lest he couldn't get his legs moving again.

He did pause long enough to unhook the field glasses from the saddle horn and take a look around. A quarter mile to the north he could make out the sharp black line of shadow marking a dry wash. These arroyos carried runoff of flash floods to the river, grooving themselves deeper as they approached the Colorado. It wasn't far now.

Boom!

The blast of a rifle shattered the stillness and a slug kicked dirt beneath the mule. The startled animal jumped and took off running, jerking the reins from Sandoval's hand. The tethered burro was yanked along behind, the pack bouncing on her back.

Another bullet sprayed sand nearby. Sandoval dove and rolled, losing himself in the black shadow beneath a big mesquite bush. He cursed, seeing his mule and burro disappearing over a rise of ground. His carbine was in the saddle sheath. He still had the field glasses and his loaded Colt.

No more shots came. The moon had disappeared and he was

well hidden. Now what? The firing had come from somewhere to the east, which meant the shooter was still behind him. He rolled over, carefully wiped off the lenses of the field glasses, put them to his eyes, and swept the surrounding area. But the darkness and his low angle prevented him from seeing anything.

Now that the moonlight was gone and he was afoot, he'd make for the arroyo and follow it to the river. He knew his animals were thirsty and would also go for the water they could probably smell. It couldn't be more than a few hundred yards away.

He pulled his Colt, blew any dust or sand out of the works, and tested the action to be sure everything was in order. He waited several minutes until he was calm again, then crawled out from under the mesquite. Crouching, he sprinted from the cover of one bush to another, knowing the shooter probably couldn't see him well enough by starlight to take a shot. But Sandoval was taking no more chances.

He purposely had not drunk any water for the past several hours, electing to preserve what was left in the leather water bag. But now the bag was gone with his mule, and that fact made him thirstier than ever. His mouth and throat were dry, and the fear of his attacker seemed to be drying him out even more.

Some fifty yards farther along, he reached the edge of the arroyo. Taking one last look around, he eased his legs over the lip of the nearly vertical bank into the blackness. Gripping a small mesquite, he let himself down, feeling with his feet for some solid footing below him. He wished he could see what was down there; it would be a disaster to fall and break a leg. There'd been no recent rain, so the deep ditch should be dry. He could only trust to luck that no poisonous desert critter was sheltering in the bottom of this arroyo.

He always carried stick matches dipped in paraffin for

waterproofing. He'd have to chance a light. When he was five feet below the lip of the arroyo, he dug out one of these matches and struck it on the metal of his Colt, cupping his hand around the flame to keep it from being seen from above.

The arroyo was at least ten feet deep, the bottom dry sand. In the few seconds he had to look before the match flared out, he saw dead brush and grass caught on exposed roots along both sides.

He paused in the darkness to catch his breath and assess his situation. Then he raked down some of the dry brush and shoved it ahead of him into a small pile on the bottom. He slid on down the sloping side, then felt for more brush to add to the pile. Pausing to catch his breath, he wondered if he'd made enough noise to pinpoint his location. He hoped so, as he struck another match and held it to the dry grass, which flared up immediately.

Throwing a larger piece of dry saguaro skeleton on the fire, he used the fire to light his way and padded softly away along the bottom, heading for the river. A diversion. If the pursuer was naive enough to sit and watch a fake campfire, then let him. But Sandoval didn't think the light from the arroyo would fool the shooter for long.

Sixty yards later, the light was dimmed by distance and the dying flames. A slight bend in the dry wash cut off all remaining illumination, and Sandoval drew his Colt and slowed in the blackness. He sensed the arroyo was becoming deeper and narrower. Without his animals to care for, Sandoval was freed up to move at will, and now felt he was the equal of this unseen gunman. Every minute or so, he paused to listen intently. No sound penetrated the narrow arroyo. If he expected his ruse to work and give him time to escape, he dared not strike a match that would betray his position. If this stalker was as smart as Sandoval had to assume he was, the man could be out-thinking and out-maneuvering him even now. The thought sent a chill up his back. He stumbled in the blackness, and put out his hand against the dirt bank to steady himself, hoping the slight rattle of loose rocks hadn't been as loud as it sounded to him.

Sandoval's knee-high desert moccasins enhanced his natural ability to glide softly. He'd learned to rely on his keen senses of sight, smell, and hearing.

The river was near, but he didn't hurry. He shuffled along quietly, feeling for obstacles.

He paused again. Something wasn't right. What? The silence was so loud it made his ears ring. Was there a breeze up at ground level to herald the coming dawn? He sensed an ominous presence. Some animal in this arroyo ahead of him? Maybe he was about to step on a rattler. He breathed deeply, then eared back the hammer of his Colt. The triple click was loud in the silence. He started forward, arms outstretched. His toe caught on a piece of driftwood, and he pitched forward, tucking his left arm to roll when he hit.

Boom!

The roar and flash lit up the arroyo. Sandoval landed hard on a flat rock, and his own gun went off. He instantly rolled left, cocking and firing upward. He dimly heard clatter and scuffling. He jumped to his feet, turned his ankle, and staggered into a pile of dead brush. Two shots roared an instant apart. In that brilliant flash, Sandoval saw his assailant and fired again in the sudden dark. Blinding light blinked out, but he caught a glimpse of a man falling against the dirt wall.

Sandoval dropped to his knees, gasping, Colt ready, but no more shots came. He was partially deafened by the explosions in the confined space. All he could hear was his own heart pounding in his ears. Nothing moved.

Shaking, he fumbled for a match and struck it on his revolver. He set the match to a clump of dead grass and brush nearby.

The light flared up, catching the tinder and sticks. Holding his Colt, he stepped carefully over the rifle on the ground and looked at the face of a man lying on his back, head against the sloping dirt bank. Nobody he knew. He reached down and checked the carotid artery for a pulse. The man was dead.

Sandoval reached back for a blazing stick from the brush pile and held the stick closer. Then something stirred in his memory. Last year a bounty hunter had tried to take him in for the $5,000 reward. Technically, Sandoval was still a wanted man with a price on his head.

What was this man's name? Breem. That was it—Breem Canto, the bandy-legged shotgun guard. Sandoval had been freed from Canto's custody by Marc Charvein, who'd wounded this man. Breem Canto had apparently recovered and come after him again, and decided to take him dead, rather than risk taking him alive.

Sandoval straightened up and drew a deep breath, then licked his dry lips. It was over now. He was as thirsty as he'd ever been. And his left arm hurt like hell. He'd tucked his forearm against his side when he fell hard on a flat rock. He moved his left hand. Pain. He touched his forearm with his right hand. Pain. The bone was cracked or broken above his left wrist. He thanked God he was right-handed.

What now? He checked the man's pockets, and took a billfold that contained some identification and twenty-three dollars in greenbacks. Then he picked up the man's rifle—a new 1886 model Winchester. With one last look he stepped over the sprawled legs and started again toward the river. The buzzards would have the remains of Breem Canto picked clean before night fell again.

Ten minutes later he began to distinguish his surroundings. He could barely see where he placed his feet. He glanced up and saw the sky paling as dawn approached.

A half-hour later, he spotted the water of the Colorado River ahead, rolling its brown current along.

Emerging finally from the deep arroyo, he waded into a patch of willows to slake his thirst in a backwater that was less gritty than the water of the main river.

Fatigue was dragging heavily at his limbs now, overpowering his body and will. He wanted nothing more than to lie down and sleep.

But one thing remained before he could do that.

He slogged on, heavy-footed. The sun finally cleared the horizon. He raised the binoculars and focused south along the river.

He smiled, feeling his dry lips crack. But he hardly noticed as he lowered the glasses, feeling rejuvenated. A hundred yards ahead his saddled mule and pack burro were grazing peacefully on the grassy bench land as if nothing had happened.

After a three-hour nap, Sandoval mounted his mule and backtracked in search of Canto's horse.

He found the bay less than two miles away, wandering along, dragging its reins and grazing on the sparse vegetation. On foot, Sandoval approached the animal, which stood quietly, apparently too tired to bolt at the sight and smell of this stranger. The animal wore a brand on his hip Sandoval had never seen before. He remounted his mule and led the horse to the river where he had picketed Lupida. He stripped the saddle and bridle from Canto's horse and turned the animal loose. It could survive on its own—possibly join some herd of wild mustangs. Or, there was enough human traffic along this river road that a traveler might find and take him. Even if someone identified the horse as Canto's, who would know what became of him? If his remains were found, scavengers would not have left enough of the body to show he'd been shot. There'd been no head wound, and consequently, no skull damage.

Watching the bay cropping the grass near the river, Sandoval wondered what to do with the horse gear. Finally, using his one good arm, he heaved the saddle, blanket, and bridle up onto his shoulder, lugged them back to the arroyo, and dumped them in. A waste of a good saddle, but it couldn't be helped. The billfold he emptied of its greenbacks, then buried the leather wallet in the sand. The big bore Winchester was too valuable to throw away. He'd sell or trade it somewhere in a remote location where it would never be traced to Breem Canto. Satisfied for the moment, he gathered up his animals and started south for Yuma.

CHAPTER 6

"How does that feel?" Doctor Vance asked, securing the last small buckle on the canvas sleeve.

"A lot better than it did," Sandoval said. "Pretty tight, though."

He held up his left forearm encased in a thick canvas sleeve reinforced by whalebone strips and fastened by leather straps.

Doctor Vance loosened it slightly. "It's still swollen some. You can adjust it later. You did a pretty fair job splinting it, using only one hand."

"It was awkward. Managed to hack off a couple small limbs to use. They were kinda heavy but they stiffened my arm for two days 'til I could get to Yuma." He swung the brace down to his side. "Will it heal straight?"

"I think the ends of the bone are slightly misaligned, but not enough to worry about. A simple fracture straight across the radius." He placed a forefinger across his own wrist to indicate the spot. "If the break occurred more than two days ago, it's already started to heal. Calcium will form around the spot and it'll be stronger than before."

"Do I keep this on all the time?"

"You can take it off to wash, but be careful and don't bend your wrist. Best to have someone help you."

"How will I know when it's healed?"

"You'll know. Probably four weeks or less." He rolled down his sleeves. "Did you fall off a horse?"

"No, I tripped on a root in the dark." The truth, but no details. "What do I owe you?"

"Two dollars, counting the brace."

"Mind taking it in gold dust?"

Doctor Vance turned from closing his black leather bag.

"I'm a prospector," Sandoval went on. "Haven't been to town for a while to have my samples assayed, so I'm out of cash. If you want to go down the street to the bank with me, I can convert this little bag of dust to coin."

Vance gave a dismissive wave of his hand. "Pay me next time you're in."

"Doctor, you and I both know we'll probably never see each other again. And I believe a man should be paid for his skills." He let his encased arm swing down gently to his side. "Only by Providence did I come into this particular saloon for a beer. And it was not by chance the bartender pointed you out eating your lunch at a table twenty feet away. He even let us use this back room. Where *is* your office?"

"I'm a military surgeon; don't have a regular office. I'm on salary and, truth be told, two dollars won't make me or break me," Vance said.

"I'd really feel better if you'd let me pay you."

"Next time you have a chance to help somebody out, do it. We're all in this together."

"Well, many thanks for your generosity."

Doctor Vance picked up his bag. "Everything evens out. Three days ago, a Mexican woman gave me a gold planchet for treating her husband. It's worth a lot more than my services."

"A gold planchet?" Sandoval's curiosity was piqued as they walked out through the saloon.

"A flat disc with no markings." He paused. "Well, actually this one does have a cross stamped on one side, and an arrow on the other."

They went out through the swinging doors and paused beneath the roof on the boardwalk.

"As a prospector, you have a feel for gold. Here, take a look and tell me if it's genuine." He motioned for them to step around the corner of the building off the street.

Vance withdrew the disc from his pocket and held it out for Sandoval to see.

"A bit crude," Sandoval picked it up. "Could be some miner just hand forged it to use in place of dust. If it's pure, it could be weighed on a scale. Seems to be about as heavy as a nugget this size."

Vance shrugged. "Odd thing about it, the Mexican villagers are poor as field mice. Either the woman didn't know the worth, or it's only gold-plated."

"An assayer could test it."

"Hate to destroy it just to find out," the doctor said. "Maybe I'll hang onto it as a curiosity. Might make a good watch fob."

"Maybe it was stolen from some church; there's a Christian cross on it."

"Maybe. Or perhaps it's actually an X instead of a cross. Some superstitious person could have stamped it on there as a charm to ward off devils or witches. But there's a circle cutting the arms of this cross. I have no idea if there's any significance to the arrow on the other side. Seriously doubt any of the Apaches in this area put it there."

"The woman who gave it to you—did you ask her about it?"

"No. She was in shock at the time. Her husband had been gravely wounded by some *bandidos,* and I wasn't sure he was going to live." He paused, as if reluctant to say more. "But one of the young *peónes* in the village who came over the border to fetch me said the disc was delivered to this poor family by a masked nightrider."

"A what?"

"That's what he said." Vance shrugged. "Told me this same masked rider wearing a black cape comes every month during a full moon and has put valuable gold discs just like this in the hands of other poor villagers."

"Sounds like someone having fun play-acting a medieval adventure," Sandoval said.

"But they're playing with real gold."

Sandoval didn't know what to say. He was surprised, but flattered that this doctor would feel comfortable confiding in him. "Some wealthy *patrón* making a game of dispersing his gold to the poor, instead of simply donating it to charity?" He shook his head. "A wild guess. I don't know. It's a mystery, sure enough. I've heard of revolutionaries buying the loyalty of common people who have barely enough to keep body and soul together."

"Yes," Vance nodded, "and most men who start revolutions are idealists, who tend to be more romantic than practical. That might account for the way the gold is dispensed." He pocketed the disc. "But this is idle speculation. I mainly wanted you to verify it's actually gold."

"Appears so. Heavy for its size, and soft enough to have small nicks and scratches from handling. But I don't know what to make of the circumstances."

The two men went to the hitching rail.

"Apparently, the word of the gold leaked out," Vance continued, lowering his voice as two men passed them and entered the saloon. "Robbers trying to force the family to give up this mysterious treasure were the ones who shot the man I treated. I don't know if his wife had more of the discs, but she acted as if she wanted to get rid of this one because it had brought bad luck down on her family and nearly cost the life of her husband."

"Well, Doc, I hope you find the answer to this riddle. Where can I find you later to pay you?"

"I live down near the border in a cabin roughly forty miles south of Fort Huachuca."

"If I get over that way, I'll leave your two dollars with someone at the fort." He thrust out his good hand. "Meanwhile, I'm in your debt. Can I at least buy you a drink?"

"No, thanks. I have to meet a colleague at the train depot." He pulled loose the reins of his Morgan from the hitching rail and heaved himself into the buggy.

Sandoval, feeling more confident using his injured arm now that it was protected by the whalebone brace, retrieved his burro and mule from the hitching rail and led them away toward the nearest livery.

CHAPTER 7

Sandoval awoke to the sound of thunder. He thought of his animals. They were sheltered in the livery. A good morning to sleep in. He rolled over to recapture his interrupted dream. A bed with clean sheets in a hotel room—what luxury after bedding down on the hard ground!

Boom! Boom! Boom!

The thunder was louder this time, and regular. He finally recognized the sound of someone pounding on his door. He reached with his good hand for the holstered Colt conversion, hanging on the bedpost.

He rolled over on his back and swung his feet to the floor, cocking the pistol.

Padding barefoot to the door, he called, "Who is it?"

"An old friend from Lodestar."

The voice was familiar and there could be only one male friend from Lodestar. But still he was cautious as he turned the key he'd left in the lock, then edged the door open, gun in hand.

"I thought you were always up and gone by this hour," Marc Charvein greeted him.

"Ahhh! Marc." Sandoval felt a rush of welcome relief to see his old friend. He let down the hammer of his Colt and tossed it onto the bed. "I'm glad to see you're not the law or a bounty hunter."

They hugged each other.

"You're thinner than ever," Charvein said, stepping back and looking him up and down. "You must be living on deer mouse and fresh air."

"Too busy to have much of an appetite these days." He reached for his pants on a chair.

"What made you think I was the law or a bounty hunter? And what happened to your arm?"

"It's a long story."

"I have time." He took a seat on the bed while Sandoval finished dressing and relating details of the bushwhacker who stalked him. He finished with the deadly confrontation in the dark arroyo.

"By damn—Breem Canto!" Charvein burst out. "I'd almost forgotten about him."

"So had I, and it nearly cost me. A man on the dodge has to keep looking over his shoulder all the time. There might be others out there still hunting me."

"Not likely, but I'll circulate the story through the local marshal's office to get rid of those old wanted posters and take you off their list, since you officially died during a shootout in Lodestar, Nevada, last year."

"Will they believe you? I'm still wanted for killing my poor wife, even though it was accidental. And for wounding Deputy Marshal Buck Rankin, who was raping her." He paused. "Even though Buck's now food for worms in the Lodestar cemetery."

"I'm a reputable citizen, working for Wells Fargo. I think the local marshal will believe I was a witness to your demise. You're old news, anyway. There are a lot hotter cases and worse bad men on their list in the territory."

"I'm hungry. Let's go get some breakfast."

"You have any other clothes?"

"Huh?" Sandoval glanced down at his smoky, greasy buckskins, desert moccasins, and ragged shirt. His tattered straw hat lay on the chair.

"You look like a half-breed Mexican peasant. In case anyone is still looking for you, it'd be a good idea to change your appearance. I have money. Before we eat, let me buy you some clothes, and take you to a barbershop. You don't grow whiskers, but you do need a haircut. You'll look like a different man."

"I splurged last night and had a soak at a Chinese bathhouse down the street. Just didn't have any clean clothes to put on. But you don't have to buy my clothes. I have a little gold dust."

"Save it. I want you in my debt because I have a favor to ask." Charvein grinned as he reached for the doorknob.

"What about this?" Sandoval held up the forearm brace.

"That shouldn't matter."

"How did you find me?"

"I went to the livery to see what horses were available to rent. Saw your burro and mule, Lupida and Jeremiah. There's no mistaking them. Asked a few questions and then started checking the hotels within walking distance."

The men went down the stairs and through the small lobby. Sandoval glanced warily around to make sure he kept any other men in sight, automatically evaluating them for potential danger. "What are you renting a horse for?" he asked as Charvein pointed toward a dry goods store down the street. "I thought you were working for Wells Fargo on the Southern Pacific."

"I am. Just checking to see if they have a durable mount available."

An hour later, they were seated near an open window at a restaurant overlooking the Colorado River putting away a late breakfast of bacon, eggs, and fried potatoes.

"Even with this broken arm, I feel like a new man." Sandoval rubbed a prickly hair near one ear where the barber's brushed talcum had failed to remove it. The soft cotton, collarless shirt, and whipcord pants seemed to caress his skin. For the first time in months, he was even wearing socks that cushioned his feet inside the turned-down moccasins.

"Amazing what a grubby existence a man can get used to over time," Charvein said as he spread prickly pear jelly on his toast, "especially living on the fringe of society."

Sandoval made no reply as he flexed the fingers of his left hand, then slightly loosened the straps on the canvas brace. He took a deep breath and sipped his coffee.

"Changes your appearance, too," Charvein added.

"You think somebody's still after me?"

Charvein shrugged. "Doubt it. Breem Canto was probably one of a kind. Persistent. I'm surprised he didn't come gunning for me for wounding him."

"There's no reward for shooting *you.*"

"If anyone happens to find Canto's remains, is there anything at that site that can tie his death to you?"

"Don't think so. I probably left a few Apache moccasin tracks in that soft sand. And I shot him with my Colt. Even if someone were to find the bullet, there's no way to trace it. My old open-top conversion revolver takes a common .44 cartridge. First spring downpour that comes along, a flash flood gushing down that arroyo will wash whatever the buzzards and varmints haven't finished into the Colorado. Might find his saddle and bedroll, though."

Charvein nodded. "People disappear in this wild country all the time. Breem Canto was a loner. I doubt if anyone will come looking for him. If they do, and even stumble across his gear, there's no link to you that I can think of. As a bounty hunter, he also went after others who had a price on their heads. I think you can take a deep breath now. You look so different from your wanted poster and your old self, no bounty hunter would recognize you. I *know* you and I would hardly think you're the same man I woke up this morning. But there's another reason you need to look a lot less like a desert rat."

"What's that?"

"I want to hire you. But my boss has the final say about it and I don't want him to turn you down because you resemble a Mexican tramp."

Sandoval didn't know what was coming, but was wary. "You and I've worked together before, and it usually involves getting my hide scuffed up."

"You'd rather go on starving and baking in the desert for a few grains of color?"

"The more I see of humans, the better I like animals." He thought of his many months of solitude in the ghost town of Lodestar, Nevada, before Charvein showed up, tracking train robbers. What followed had changed his life.

"Suit yourself." Charvein shrugged, dunking a crust of toast into the runny egg yolk. "But I've been given leeway to hire a man I trust. The pay's decent, and it could work into a permanent job. You'll be in the employ of Wells Fargo."

"Why hire me? I have no skills, except maybe as a prospector and a survivor. What's the job?"

"The Wells Fargo express car has been robbed several times over the past few months. I had a gun stuck in my face a week ago, and they got away with the contents of the safe. I want you to help me figure out and catch whoever is responsible."

"I'm not a lawman."

"My district superintendent will make it worth your while. His job is on the line and he's coming close to retirement. If I can't somehow put a stop to it, I might be unemployed, too. He thinks since I was a railroad detective years ago, I can unravel the mystery. In terms of age and experience, I'm the senior express messenger on the run between Los Angeles and El Paso. If I don't put a stop to it quick, or at least find out who's behind it, my boss'll be forced to admit defeat and call in the Pinkertons. And the big shots at Wells Fargo think everything should be handled internally. Makes them look bad if they have to ask for outside help."

Sandoval drained his coffee mug and said nothing, weighing his options. "I'll give it a try on one condition."

Charvein waited.

"That you have no expectations."

"I mainly want you to watch my back; I can rely on you not to panic at the sound of gunfire. You also have a level head and an instinct for survival. This job will involve riding the express car with me, and maybe one other guard. You're not considered outside help; you're just another part-time employee."

Sandoval smiled. "If that's all that's required, then I'm your man." He paused and grew serious. "What about my burro and mule?"

"I'll pay to have them stabled for a couple of weeks right where they are, if that's suitable."

Sandoval nodded. "Fair enough." He pushed his chair back from the table. "When do I start?"

CHAPTER 8

The Southern Pacific locomotive ground to a halt in a burst of steam at its last water stop before following the mainline into Los Angeles County.

Marc Charvein used a large key from his belted key ring to let himself out the end door of the express car, the spring lock snapping the iron door shut behind him.

"Dull trip so far." Sandoval greeted him, stepping back into the shade of the downcurving roof.

"About what I expected, since we're westbound." Charvein leaned on the iron guardrail and breathed deeply of the evening breeze, which carried a taint of wood smoke from the locomotive's balloon stack. He was hardly aware that his senses were continuously probing everything around him.

"All the robberies have taken place on eastbound runs," Sandoval said.

Charvein listened to the soft panting of the locomotive and the garbled voices of the crew at the water tower ahead. Anytime the train was stopped, he was uneasy. "Yeah, that's what the reports showed. We carry more gold out of California. Not much valuable cargo going west."

"And they take only the contents of the safe—nothing big," Sandoval went on.

"They always come out of the desert on horseback with no wagon or pack mules," Charvein said, "so there's no way they could carry off anything big or heavy. Lightning strikes. Fast and mobile. Hit and retreat."

The two men were silent for several seconds. "There's one shipper who's a regular." Sandoval seemed hesitant to point out the obvious.

"Yeah, I know—Grindell Jewelers. That firm is fast becoming the biggest jewelry maker in California. They even own their own gold mine, *Halloran's Luck*, which has continued to produce for five years. Mighty convenient. There are other shippers, too, but none with the volume or regularity of Grindell."

"Wells Fargo must be taking quite a loss just on that one shipper, if your company has to reimburse for everything stolen."

Charvein nodded. "Yeah." He felt down and out of sorts. Since Sandoval had hired on, ten days earlier, nothing out of the routine had occurred. And a further study of the robbery reports had shown no further discernible pattern of holdups. Charvein had taken the precaution of stationing Sandoval on the outside platform of the car, himself inside the locked interior, and the young Bob Billings on the outside platform at the other end of the car. "That way, we won't all be trapped inside. One or both of you can see any danger coming a ways off and get 'em in a crossfire before they can get close." It seemed like a logical precaution. Whether that rearrangement or just happenstance had prevented any further holdups was unknown by anyone but the robbers themselves.

Charvein had thoroughly grounded Sandoval in all the known details of the string of robberies.

"Of course," Sandoval said, as if it were perfectly obvious. "Whoever's behind this is a romantic, as well as a practical bandit—a highwayman who wants to be famous and talked about. He—or they—want the notoriety. I'd bet the gang is aware the papers have dubbed them the Border Brigands."

"Could be," Charvein replied as they sat poring over the written reports in the Wells Fargo office that day a week earlier.

"People love to be noticed," Sandoval had said. "The center of attention. Any criminal could probably remain unknown, if that's what he really wanted. But where would be the fun and excitement in that, if you could get away clean with no one hunting you?"

"Humans are a strange breed," Charvein had admitted.

A short blast of the steam whistle signaled the train was watered up and ready to get underway, shattering Charvein's musings. He straightened up from leaning on the railing. "Go on inside. I'll relieve you out here for a while."

Sandoval had his key in the lock when he paused and turned back. "Where is this Grindell Jewelers company headquartered?"

"Downtown Los Angeles somewhere."

"If we have a day layover, you think it would help to pay them a visit?"

Charvein considered this. "Let's try it. Maybe we can catch the owner in the office. Dress up a bit and pretend to be a customer inspecting their operation for a buyer back east. Maybe we can get a notion of what this owner is like. Maybe nose around a little, ask a few questions, keep our heads down. Might learn something useful." He smiled grimly. "Wouldn't be the first time a shipper has hired bandits to steal the goods and return them, while the shipper splits the reimbursement Wells Fargo paid out for the loss."

They braced themselves as the train jerked into motion, but Sandoval still hesitated at the heavy door, a thoughtful look on his face. "You know, the description of the items stolen didn't strike me as worth the effort and danger. Is that gold jewelry really so valuable?"

"I wondered the same thing," Charvein said, more satisfied than ever he'd hired his old friend, whose powers of observation were superior to his own. "The gold content makes up the major portion of the value—the workmanship and jewels, the rest. All the losses put together, counting the other stuff in the safe that didn't belong to Grindell, probably totaled seventy thousand."

"A goodly sum. Well worth it, I guess." He unlocked the door and went inside as the train began to pick up speed.

"Mister Grindell is out of town." The young man with the pince-nez and the stiff white collar barely glanced at Charvein and Sandoval who stood before his desk.

Probably his standard reply to anyone asking to see the big boss without an appointment, Charvein thought.

"We've come a long way to see him on a matter of some importance," Charvein said. "When will he be back?"

Charvein thought Sandoval, with his smooth, whiskerless skin and dark hair and features, white shirt and cravat could pass for a wealthy businessman from New Delhi, instead of a mixed-blood Indian from the Americas. His friend seemed to be swelling his chest to make the rented coat appear to fit.

"He'll be gone the rest of the week," the clerk said in a dismissive tone. "If you'd like to make an appointment, perhaps we can work you in the first week of June."

"Well, that was a waste of time," Charvein observed when they were ensconced in a day coach on their way back to Yuma.

"As long as Wells Fargo fully guarantees against any losses, why would Grindell care what happens to a shipment?" Sandoval shrugged. In deference to the heat, he had cast off his more formal business disguise in favor of well-worn canvas pants and a cotton shirt he'd carried in a leather grip that was now stowed in the overhead rack.

"Several reasons I can think of offhand." Charvein thoughtfully stared out at the dun-colored landscape sliding past at a steady thirty miles per hour. The window was closed against the dust and wood smoke. "First of all, Grindell is in business to make money—not to break even. Secondly, he's paying artisans to craft unique pieces of jewelry from gold. If he has wealthy clients or retail stores back east who want his products and he consistently fails to deliver, his customers will go elsewhere. And thirdly, I would think his pride would be hurt and his curiosity piqued. He must be getting frustrated."

" 'Frustrated' is the word I'd apply to the regional superinten-dent."

"Right you are. If we don't make some headway on this case, he'll either fire me or explode in a fit of apoplexy."

Charvein was suddenly very tired, even though he'd had a decent night's sleep in the hotel room the night before. He slouched down on the green velvet and leaned his head against the seat back, closing his eyes.

CHAPTER 9

The telegraph key in the tiny Western Union office rattled one last staccato burst and fell silent.

Dennis Dugan finished copying the message onto his pad and tapped a quick acknowledgment. Then he tore off the sheet and swung around, the swivel chair squealing in protest. He launched his stocky frame toward the door to the adjacent Southern Pacific depot.

Startled, Charvein looked up when the door slammed back against the wall. Dugan stood, glaring around the room and focused on the dispatcher Charvein was conferring with.

"Where's my runner?"

"Pablo? Dunno. He was sweeping the floor in the waiting room not five minutes ago." The balding dispatcher pulled off his green eyeshade and wiped a sleeve across his forehead as he came out from behind the grilled window.

"Something hot off the wire?" Charvein asked.

"This needs to go to Coughlin right away."

"What's up?"

Dugan blew out a deep breath, his ruddy face more flushed than usual.

"Another robbery. Cleaned out the express car safe again."

An icy ball knotted Charvein's stomach. "Anybody hurt?"

"Doesn't say. Short on details."

"Wire back and ask," Charvein said. "Where'd it happen?"

"Just east of the Mohawk Mountains where the train had to

slow on a switchback grade."

"Give me that. I'll take it to Coughlin. I need to go see the boss, anyway." He knew Coughlin would quiz him, and he was glad he had no further details at the moment.

He snatched the sheet of paper and left. When he reached the superintendent's office a block away, he discovered Coughlin had gone to lunch.

"Jared, the boss needs to see this as soon as he returns." Charvein held out the handwritten telegraph message, hesitating to place it on the clerk's desk, lest it be swallowed up by the clutter. Since Charvein had been hired on as an express car messenger several months earlier, he had yet to see the top of the clerk's desk. He didn't know how Jared Wilson functioned as efficiently as he did, given the mass of papers that were strewn about, some falling off the edges to the floor. Wilson's fresh haircut, striped red tie, and sleeve garters on his white shirt contrasted sharply with his messy workspace.

Just to be certain the young man knew the gravity of this telegram, he added, "Another express car robbery on the westbound."

"Mister Coughlin will be back in thirty-two minutes." Wilson glanced at the wall clock. "I'll see that he gets it."

Wilson was dependable so Charvein left the message, secretly relieved he could delay facing the boss's wrath. No matter that this most recent robbery had nothing to do with Charvein, Coughlin would somehow twist the news so it would seem so. He would at least blame Charvein for not ferreting out the culprits sooner.

As he walked back to the Southern Pacific depot, he hoped Dugan had received more details of the robbery. What would this do to the schedule? He and Sandoval were due to take that same train on its overnight run to Los Angeles. Was there damage to the express car? If so, the train, due to pull out of Yuma for the coast at 8:33, would likely be late.

He found Sandoval eating alone in the Harvey House next to the depot. Charvein snagged up a wooden chair with one foot, swung it around, and sat down, folding his arms across the back. "Hear the latest?"

Sandoval glanced up, but only grunted as he continued eating.

Charvein related the news.

"Same gang?" Sandoval put his fork down.

"Don't know yet. Dennis is trying to get more details."

"If so, that's the first robbery that far east."

"Longer ride to the border from there, too."

"A lot of open desert between the Mohawk Mountains and Mexico." Sandoval swabbed up the last of the brown gravy and popped the bread into his mouth. "And drier than an old man's scalp."

A Mexican boy appeared at the doorway, spotted them, and trotted to their table, waving a piece of paper. "From Señor Dugan." He handed over the yellow sheet and left.

Charvein scanned the note. Even when rushed, the Irish-born telegrapher wrote a neat hand.

"Damn!" he breathed.

Sandoval looked at him.

"Billings was wounded."

"Bad?"

Charvein shook his head. "Hit in the thigh. Apparently, he'll make it, but he won't be working for a while. The kid probably shot off his mouth and got one of those itchy-fingered robbers stirred up. He damn near did the same when I was aboard."

"Not a wise thing if you're not the one holding the gun," Sandoval observed, sipping his coffee.

"That means we're one man short now. Somebody will have to cover for him." He paused, thoughtfully. "Maybe the new messenger out of California. That'll leave us free to follow up on any leads."

"What leads?"

Charvein shrugged. "About four years back I was a railroad detective. Coughlin knows I'm the only express messenger with that kind of experience. He doesn't want to call in the Pinkertons." He paused. "Somehow this whole case has to have a common thread."

Something about these border bandits was lurking out there on the dark fringes of his consciousness, something he couldn't quite grasp. It was like trying to recall a familiar name, or trying to see a face in a dream. It kept eluding him. "I just wish we had something positive to go on."

"Did you notice that no one has been killed in any of these robberies?" Sandoval said.

"Yeah, you mentioned that before. I guess as long as they get what they're after, there's no need for killing."

"And the penalty for murder is hanging—not a prison sentence." Sandoval wiped his mouth with the napkin. "Robbery's not as likely to put man hunters on your trail."

Charvein leaned back in his chair, a toothpick in his mouth. "This gang of bandits rides out of Mexico, strikes, and runs back to their hideout across the border where they know they're safe from U.S. law."

"But they're not safe from a couple of inquisitive railroad detectives," Sandoval mused.

"I can't imagine what they could be doing with gold jewelry," Charvein said. "Why not go after gold bullion or coins? Maybe they're exporting it by ship through the Sea of Cortez."

"Jewelry is somewhat lighter to carry," Sandoval said. "But what you just said makes me wonder if the jewelry is being retained in its present form."

"What do you mean?"

"Remember I told you about that Doctor Vance, the Army surgeon who set my broken wrist?"

"Yeah?"

"When I tried to pay him in gold dust, he waved it off and said he didn't need my two dollars."

"Really?"

"Said he'd been overpaid by a woman in a tiny Mexican village last week for digging a bullet out of her husband. He showed me the gold disc she'd given him. It was a sort of homemade coin about the size of a silver dollar. Doc said it was easily worth ten times his normal fee."

"A homemade coin?"

"Obviously hand-stamped."

"Maybe the Mexicans found some ore and crafted it themselves."

"It had a cross stamped on one side and an arrow on the other. Doctor Vance said he was going to hang onto it as a keepsake."

"Did the doctor know where it originated?"

Sandoval related the tale Vance had told him of the masked nightrider distributing gold discs like this to other poor Mexicans in the area, most of whom barely had enough to eat.

"Strange," Charvein stood up. "But that's someone else's mystery to solve."

"The coin the doc showed me looked to be newly minted. I'm thinking there might be a connection between these homemade discs and the gold jewelry that's being snatched from the express cars and disappearing across the border."

"More likely somebody has hit a small vein of ore somewhere in the Sierra Madre," Charvein said. "By smelting it and making their own crude coins they can keep from carrying dust or nuggets that would attract the attention of bandits who might go after the mine. If a prospector finds a small mine in some remote area, even if he has it legally recorded, no Mexican or American law is going to keep claim jumpers from taking it if they have the firepower to do it." The two men were silent with their own thoughts for several seconds.

"Is Doctor Vance still in Yuma?" Charvein asked.

"I doubt it. He travels around and serves the various forts and army posts in the southern territory. But we can ask. He shouldn't be hard to find."

Charvein turned toward the door.

"Where you off to?"

"To ask Coughlin to replace us on the run to Los Angeles this evening," Charvein said over his shoulder. "He won't be happy about it, but he'll let us go if I tell him we have a lead. The crew coming from the east can take it on from here and maybe earn some overtime."

"You said Billings was shot."

"The new man, Jake Collins, from California, is here to get oriented. I'll let the boss worry about who to send. Besides, if the bandits already took what they wanted, unless a valuable shipment is picked up here, there won't be much to guard except maybe some big items."

Sandoval wiped his mouth on a napkin and rose from the table. "The train they hit was westbound," he said. "All the shipments up to now have been eastbound. Wonder what they took?"

Charvein paused and studied the dark, lean face of his friend. Even though Sandoval claimed to be of mixed Spanish and Incan descent, his sharper features were at odds with the depiction of those ancient people, shown in stone carvings with thicker lips and broad noses. Charvein suspected Sandoval had created his own ancestry and identity as a shield to a hostile world. For all he knew, Sandoval might be part Apache.

Charvein forced himself out of his reverie. "Well, we'll have to get a manifest to find out what was taken. Could be our theory was totally wrong about Grindell having something to do with his own shipments being stolen."

CHAPTER 10

"Wouldn't you rather have a horse to ride?" Charvein asked as the two men were saddling up in a Yuma livery two hours later.

Sandoval shook his head, tugging up a girth of the double-rigged mule saddle. "Jeremiah and I've been through a lot together. Besides, mules and burros are tougher than horses when it comes to surviving in rough terrain with little water. Lupida can carry our packs."

"If we have to hightail it out of a tight spot, it's good to have some speed."

"A trade-off," Sandoval replied. "Jeremiah isn't that slow. And I'll go for durability every time in the desert."

Charvein knew Sandoval had spent much more time alone in the desert and survived some harrowing experiences, so he silently deferred to the half-breed's judgment.

"We'll ride over the river and catch Doctor Vance before he leaves Fort Yuma." Charvein changed the subject. "Hope he can give us something positive, or point us in the right direction before we slip across the border. With any luck, this might lead to something." He flipped the stirrup down and slid his Winchester '73 lever action into the saddle sheath. He'd already checked, loaded, and holstered the top-break British .45 the wounded robber had dropped.

"You're not going to use Canto's 1886 Winchester?" Charvein asked, noting that Sandoval also had a model 1873 Winchester he'd drawn from the Wells Fargo armory.

"No. This will do me. My Marlin is a different caliber, too, and I want my Colt and rifle to use the same size ammunition."

Charvein guessed another reason Sandoval was leaving the new 1886 model behind was to divest himself of his final connection with the dead bounty hunter.

"Maybe there's a connection between the coins and the robberies, and maybe not," Sandoval said, picking up the thread of their earlier conversation. He shrugged. "Worth a shot anyway."

They led their mounts and the loaded burro out into the sunshine.

"Did Coughlin give you a hard time about taking off?" Sandoval asked as they mounted.

"Not really. I was surprised. Thought he'd raise hell, but I stretched the truth a mite when I told him we had a lead. Acted as if I was in a hurry and couldn't stop to explain. I think he was relieved. Waved me out of his office."

Dennis Dugan stepped out the door when they rode up to the depot and dismounted. He handed them a message that the delayed westbound was due to arrive by 6:30 that evening. The express car had not been damaged. "Looks as if she'll be able to pull out of here at 8:10, on schedule. No towns near the robbery site, so no posse could be organized to track the robbers," Dugan added.

Charvein handed back the telegram. "Thanks, Dennis." He pointed at the American flag flapping lazily in the breeze on a hilltop across the Colorado. "If anybody comes looking for us, we're riding over to Fort Yuma. Back by suppertime."

"The quartermaster said you wanted to see me." Doctor Vance set his black bag on his buggy seat. "Having trouble with that arm?"

"It's fine, Doc," Sandoval said, "except for trying to keep the brace clean."

"A little dirt won't matter since there's no open wound." He took hold of Sandoval's hand. "Swelling's gone. Just don't be lifting anything over a pound. And no pulling. Got it? Keep the brace strapped tight while you're up and about. You can loosen it a bit at night."

Sandoval nodded.

The doctor took the reins a private soldier was holding for him, and prepared to step up into the buggy.

Sandoval dug out a $2.50 gold piece and handed it to Vance. "For setting my arm," he said.

"I told you not to bother about that."

"I pay my debts when I can," Sandoval said, "but I do have another favor to ask. Can I take a look at that gold disc you showed me?"

Vance's quizzical look shifted to Charvein.

"It's okay. This is Mark Charvein. He's a Wells Fargo express messenger and a railroad detective. We work together."

Vance fingered the coin out of a vest pocket and handed it over.

Charvein examined it closely in the bright sunlight. "You didn't mention it was a Celtic cross," he said to Sandoval.

"A what?"

"The arms of the cross are enclosed in a circle," Charvein said. "Probably fashioned that way centuries ago to give it strength and rigidity. Celtic crosses are common on Irish gravestones and architecture," Charvein added. He turned the coin over and looked at the simple arrow, the fletching and the point made with straight lines, like a child's drawing. The edge of the disc was not raised. "Pretty simple. No milling on the edge, either, like a government-minted coin would have." This practice had originated many decades before to keep dishonest merchants and individuals from shaving off slivers of the precious metal before passing the coin on.

Charvein handed the coin to Sandoval, who passed it back to Vance.

"What's this about?" the doctor asked. "You believe this was stolen?"

Charvein shook his head. "No reason to think so. Just trying to get a line on several shipments of gold jewelry stolen from the Wells Fargo express car over the past few months. The robbers took off toward the Mexican border."

"Did you tell him where I got this?" Vance directed his question at Sandoval.

Charvein nodded. "That's why I wanted to look at it."

"Did you save that Mexican man's life?" Sandoval put in.

"The one who was shot? Oh, he lived all right. Probably due more to luck or Providence than to anything I was able to do. He's past the crisis, but he'll be a few weeks healing."

"You say the man's wife gave you the coin in payment?" Charvein prompted.

Vance nodded. "That's right. I was reluctant to take it since the people in that village are so desperately poor. And it's worth far more than my fee. But she insisted. Said the coin had brought them nothing but bad luck."

"Tell him what the boy told you about the masked nightrider," Sandoval said.

Doctor Vance repeated the story the teen had related about a mysterious nightrider who delivered coins just like this to other villagers, each month during a night of the full moon, especially to families who'd experienced some severe hardship. "Evidently, the word got out and some *bandidos* swooped down on those poor folks and were looking for the coins when this Mexican man resisted and was shot for his trouble."

"Where is this village?" Charvein asked.

"I'd be careful about riding down there," Doctor Vance said. "Those people see two strangers, they're liable to shoot first and look for identification on your bodies later. They're understandably on edge."

Charvein nodded. "We'll take all precautions."

"Anyone asking about the origin of those coins is likely to be labeled an outlaw and a bandit."

"You think the villagers, themselves, know who is giving out these coins?"

"If they do, they were careful to hide the fact from me." He squinted at them from under the gray hat brim. "The village is named San Felipe and the wounded man was Juan Fortuna. The village is just across the border in a valley only a few miles from my cabin." He gave some general directions.

Charvein wished he had a map with him. He tried to visualize the general area. "Hmm . . . that would be somewhere due south of Ajo."

Doctor Vance nodded. "There is nothing to mark the international boundary there. And I don't think San Felipe is marked on any map. The nearest Mexican village is Sonoita, but that's probably twenty miles to the east, near the stream of the same name." He grabbed an upright brace and swung into his buggy seat. "Anything else I can help you with? I have to make the upbound riverboat to get to Ehrenberg. The *Mohave* is due to pull out in an hour and I have to stable my horse at the livery first."

"What's your theory about these coins?" Charvein asked.

Vance shook his head. "Beats anything I ever heard. I thought at first it was some revolutionary group trying to win friends among the *peónes* before starting a coup. But that's just a guess. Don't really know. I haven't been able to get back to my house since then. Could be something else has happened. If you go to San Felipe and speak to the Fortunas, you can say you know me, but be very diplomatic. I have the friendship of the villagers and don't want them to think I somehow betrayed their trust, and brought more trouble down on their heads."

"Don't worry."

Vance turned his horse and slapped the reins over the Morgan's back. The buggy rolled downslope, away from the post toward the road and the Colorado River bridge.

The dust from its passing still hung in the air when Charvein gave a deep sigh.

"What's wrong?" Sandoval looked up from untying Jeremiah and Lupida from the shade of the nearby hitching rail.

"I was planning to head south into Mexico along the Colorado River, but Doc Vance says this village is many miles east of here."

"We can catch the eastbound freight out of Yuma about sundown," Sandoval said. "Drop off at Gila Bend and head south."

Charvein stepped into the saddle without replying, and tugged his horse around. He rode away, aware that Sandoval had mounted his mule and was following, the burro on a long tether. Charvein led the way back across the bridge, noting the green current flowing beneath. Now, in early April, the Colorado was rising, swollen by snowmelt from the Grand Canyon plateau miles to the north.

A half-hour later, after a stop at the Wells Fargo office, they rode up to the Southern Pacific depot and dismounted, tying their animals near the water trough in the shade of the overhanging roof.

Charvein dug into his saddlebags and drew out a rolled, large-scale map, printed on oilcloth.

It was only 2:35 p.m., Charvein noted by the big wall regulator as they crossed the empty waiting room that smelled faintly of wood smoke and old cigars. Pushing open the door to the adjacent Harvey House restaurant, Charvein breathed deeply of the aroma of fried chicken. An eastbound passenger train was due in forty-five minutes. But, at the moment, only two men occupied separate tables in the spacious dining room. Charvein selected a round table close to a window for plenty of outside light.

A uniformed waitress took their order for coffee *au lait*. *How long will it be before I can order cream in my coffee again?* Charvein thought as the waitress departed. He thrust the thought from his mind and unrolled the map on top of the table.

"Before you showed up, here's where we were when the train was hit in March," he stated, putting a finger on a blank spot. "In the middle of the sand dunes about thirty miles west of Yuma."

Sandoval scooted his chair around so he could see the map right-side up. "Yeah."

"Two men. I wounded one of them before the other threw a stick of dynamite into the car. They headed south through the dunes. No water or shade or anyplace to hide out for miles."

"The border looks to be less than three miles south of the rail line at that point," Sandoval said. "Once they crossed over, they could have cut east toward the river."

"Just what I was thinking. They had canteens on their saddles, but weren't carrying any water for the horses. You know of any springs or seeps straight south?"

Sandoval pursed his thin lips for a moment. "I was down that way only once, as a boy with my uncle many years ago." He shook his head. "I think there was one small stream running toward the Colorado."

"If the bandits turned west for twenty miles or so, they'd run into the foothills of the Sierra de Juárez, part of the mountain chain that forms the backbone of the Baja Peninsula. Looks to be some foliage in the higher elevations. Could be a spring or tanks in there. Don't see any villages marked on the map."

Sandoval nodded. "Doc Vance said San Felipe wasn't marked either."

"I'd guess they'd fight shy of contact with natives or any villages," Charvein continued. "But we could ride south along the Colorado River, question any Mexicans we run across to see if we can pick up their trail. But San Felipe, where Doc Vance got that coin, is more than a hundred miles east of here." He slid his finger along the international boundary to a spot just south of Ajo. He paused to let Sandoval scan the wide gap on the map. "The shortest way there is to ride east by south along the El Camino del Diablo."

Before he even finished speaking, Sandoval was shaking his head. "That would be suicide. It's not called El Camino del Diablo for nothing. I know that area. Just miles and miles of heat and sand with no water. Many men and animals have died trying to cross there. Even Apaches avoid that route as summer comes on."

"The road passes near the Tinajas Altas."

"True, and we had a wet spring, so those high tanks in the rocks might still be holding some water," Sandoval said. "But, do you want to gamble our lives on that slim chance? And any water we might find there would be scummy and full of wigglers. A sure way to bring on sickness, unless it is strained and boiled."

"Okay, then, the best way to reach this village of San Felipe is to grab a freight all the way to Gila Bend, seventy-five miles north of the border, then ride south from there."

"Much safer," Sandoval agreed. "And we would start out fresh. The train would take only half a day to reach Gila Bend, then we'd have a few wells and springs scattered along the way south."

Charvein was silent for a moment, translating the inches before him into the miles they represented. The lines and colored topographic features on the map made it look easy. But, in his mind's eye he could see the dry, sandy bed of the Gila River, snaking east from Yuma toward the rail stop at Gila Bend. Why was it even called a river? His own limited experience in the Sonoran desert had burned a vision into his memory of blue-gray stony mountains floating on shimmering heat waves, never coming closer, no matter how many hours or days a traveler plodded toward them. This was no eastern landscape with hills clothed in green trees and clear streams purling over pebbled beds. Here humans were only insects in the eternal dusty distance. What good to rush off into the desert chasing a gang of robbers if you were also rushing off to leave your desiccated flesh for the vultures?

"You're right, of course," he finally admitted. "I was just trying to make this trip a little easier."

"There is no easy way, *amigo.*"

"Yeah, that's one reason nobody has come close to tracking these robbers." The enormity of this venture was beginning to depress him.

"Mostly it is because American lawmen have no jurisdiction south of the line. Officially, no one can chase them," Sandoval went on. "And the Mexican *rurales* have problems of their own with *bandidos.* If this gang has not broken any laws in Mexico, they are probably being ignored—if anyone even knows who or where they are." Sandoval placed his arm brace atop the table as a hot breeze from the open window began to flutter the map.

Sandoval was calm and logical, seemed to always be thinking and calculating the odds. Those qualities had kept him alive the last few years when he was a wanted man hiding in the ghost town of Lodestar, Nevada, and later as a lone prospector tracked by a man-killing bounty hunter. Only once had Charvein seen him lose control of his emotions—when he had run, armed and shouting, into the streets of Lodestar, to challenge ex-marshal

Buck Rankin. Two years earlier the former lawman had been in the act of raping Sandoval's wife and Sandoval tried to shoot him. But, in the melee, Sandoval had accidentally killed his own wife, and only wounded Rankin. But all that was behind them now, and the body of Rankin was in an unmarked grave in Lodestar.

Studying his friend's lean, beardless face, Charvein wondered once again what lay behind those dark, hooded eyes. Sandoval was a small man, but must have been put together with piano wire. He was as tough and durable as a century plant. Charvein knew little of his background except what Sandoval had cautiously let slip. But Charvein was comfortable confiding in him. Had he been a gambler, Sandoval's poker face would never have betrayed his hand. They were an unlikely pair, he and this wiry half-breed. They'd saved each other's lives more than once, beginning in the ruins of a dusty Nevada ghost town. And it was anyone's guess what lay ahead for them.

CHAPTER 11

Amid a crash of breaking dishes, Lucinda Barkley tore off her apron and threw it down, hands shaking.

Several diners looked up.

"What's wrong?" Her best friend, Frances Cain, hurried over to put an arm around Lucy's shoulders and guide her toward the windows of the Los Angeles Harvey House Restaurant. The early afternoon sunshine was pouring in, lighting up the white tablecloths.

"I can't take it anymore, Fran," she tried to steady her trembling voice.

Frances glanced around, blond hair falling over her shoulder. "Is that same man putting his hands on you?" she asked quietly. "The one with the slick black hair and the stickpin in his tie?"

"Yeah."

"Who is he?"

"Adolphus Grindell. Some rich, oily character who thinks all Harvey girls are fair game."

"Well, a lot of the waitresses meet husbands by working here," Fran said calmly. "I've had two proposals myself, one of them serious." She shook her head. "But I wasn't that desperate." She glanced over her shoulder again. "He's leaving. All wet and red in the face," she added with a chuckle.

"I threw a bowl of soup on him and slapped him—hard," she said. "I've just had enough." She felt her eyes tearing up. "Oh, God, here comes Mister Rawlins. I saw him watching from the kitchen door."

"Brace up," Fran whispered. "I'll back you."

The two women turned to face the chubby dining room supervisor who came huffing up, puffing out his rosy, beardless cheeks. He glared at Lucy, round eyes magnified by the lenses in his wire-rimmed spectacles. For some odd reason, Lucy noted the pomade gleaming from the man's brown hair, which was parted in the middle and slicked back, resembling the bullet head of a snake.

"I saw you strike that customer," he finally managed to articulate. "Are you out of your mind? We don't do that here!"

Lucy didn't reply, but Fran said, "The man was pawing her."

"I don't care what he was doing! There's no way he could rape you in a public place. Anything less than that is dismissed without a word. You understand?" He face was flushed.

A young Mexican boy was cleaning up the broken crockery. The other patrons had gone back to eating.

"That's the third time he's done that this week," Lucy finally said.

"Harvey House has a reputation to maintain," Rawlins blustered. "The customers *always* come first. We . . . you are to look neat and presentable and to show every courtesy to our patrons."

"He . . ."

"I don't want to hear any excuses. That man is Adolphus Grindell, a very wealthy gold merchant. Of all people to be rude to!" He paused, flecks of spittle at the corners of his mouth. Lucy thought perhaps Rawlins was about to suffer a fit of apoplexy. If he did, would she just walk away and leave him lying there for someone else to assist? Her detached imagination carried her away from the scene while she continued to stare blankly at him. From somewhere, the familiar ranting rained down on her unhearing ears. A red curtain was descending

77

across her vision. She knew the feeling of uncontrolled rage.

"You've been nothing but trouble since you came here!" Rawlins almost shouted. "I'm not taking it anymore. You're fired!"

Swiftly she reached for a bowl of creamed corn left on an unbussed table nearby. The shot to the face of Mister Rawlins was dead center, and he staggered back, gasping, glasses askew, white shirt and silk tie dripping yellow. The bowl was shattered on the floor, and his shiny shoes splattered.

She strode away, reveling in a delicious satisfaction.

"Lucy, wait!" Fran Cain called after her.

"Can't talk now," she called back without turning around. "Come by my hotel tonight."

Then she was gone.

Once her mind was made up, Lucy didn't hesitate. During a quiet dinner in the hotel dining room that evening, she said her goodbyes to Fran Cain, and resisted all attempts by her good friend to dissuade her from leaving.

"I'm not going back there," she stated firmly, sipping a glass of red wine. "Even if I should want to go crawling back and begging forgiveness, Rawlins would never hire me back." She shook her head. "No, I must go on and find out what else is ahead of me."

"What are your plans?" Fran asked, her blond hair shining in the light of the overhead coal oil chandelier. "Where will you go?"

"I'll collect my savings from the bank in the morning and buy a train ticket to Yuma."

"Why Yuma?"

"That's my first stop," she replied. "Maybe see what kind of legitimate job I can find there."

"Whew! It's coming on to summer. That place is only one step from Hades when it comes to weather." Fran forked up a bite of chocolate cake.

Lucy had only a half-formed idea of trying to look up Marc Charvein, who had stopped to see her a month ago on his way to Los Angeles in his new job as a Wells Fargo messenger.

"I might look up an old friend there," she said.

"Male or female?"

"Marc Charvein. He's like an older brother to me."

"Really? Tell me about him." She smiled and signaled the waiter to bring more coffee.

Lucy struggled with her innate reserve. Why not tell her friend the story of how Charvein had rescued her in Lodestar, Nevada, the year before? So, for the next half-hour she confided the story of how she and Marc Charvein had met, how he'd saved her life, how she'd later been shot in the leg in a wild gun battle. Then, at the end, she'd saved *his* life when one of the wounded killers was about to put a knife into the sleeping Charvein.

"My God, what a story!" Fran said when the tale was done. "You were taken hostage by the escaping inmates in Carson City?"

Lucy nodded. "My life had been very dull up to that point. Guess my parents should have had a son instead of me. I always longed for adventure, but had to read stories of medieval times and battles and court intrigues, and wandering minstrels. My adventures were vicarious."

"Working in a prison warden's office doesn't sound boring," Fran said.

"Believe me, it was—until all hell broke loose. Then, for a while I would have given anything for a little boredom." She smiled, but went on to tell how she and a gambler had returned to Lodestar to dig out the stolen gold from the ruins of a dynamited church. "We made off with it in a wagon just ahead of Ezra Pitney, the mine owner who was coming to retrieve his gold. I felt I was due some compensation for the ordeal I'd been through. It was just plain stealing," she admitted, "but I was mad and I was desperate and not thinking straight. Turned out I selected the wrong man to help me."

She related how he'd gambled away much of the stolen gold in San Francisco before she took the remaining loot in the form of a gold cross and escaped, bringing it around through the Sea of Cortez and back up to Yuma. There she'd rejoined Charvein and Sandoval, the hermit from Lodestar. A final wild shootout had ensued, and the three friends had given a false story to the police, and later donated the refashioned gold cross to a mission church in California. "I'm not sure how, but I escaped the penalty of the law for theft. I'm not proud of what I did. Guess I should be thankful I'm not in prison right now for stealing and lying." Then she smiled. "But in the end, since the church got the cross, I consider it a gift in the name of Ezra Pitney, the owner. He has plenty more where that came from."

"My God, Lucy, you've had more terrifying adventures than any ten people!" Fran was wide-eyed. "And to think we've been working together for months, and I thought you were just a nice, quiet girl from a good background, maybe on the lookout for a husband, like the rest of us at the Harvey House."

Lucy sipped at the lukewarm coffee, then refilled her cup from the carafe on the table.

"Tell me more about this Marc Charvein. Is he attractive? He's certainly strong and brave. How old is he?"

Lucy tried to assess her own feelings for Charvein. There'd been no spark between them during all the things that had happened. Had she really known him less than two years? The things they'd shared seldom happened to two people in the course of a lifetime. "I think I'll look him up when I get to Yuma," she said.

"Nothing other than friendship between you?" Fran arched her eyebrows. "So he's married?"

"No. As far as I know, he's never been. I'd guess he's maybe late thirties. Maybe a bit older. Hard to tell." Although she didn't admit it, she felt Charvein knew her too well, knew her foibles and weaknesses. There was no pretending around him, and she was not comfortable with that. People, she felt, should always have a layer of cushion between them to keep from being too vulnerable. Humans could only open up to animals, who were not judgmental. But maybe men didn't think that way.

Fran was busy writing something on a slip of paper with a short pencil. "Here. This is my address. I want you to promise you'll write and tell me what happens to you. And you know where you can always find me at work, unless that little weasel, Rawlins, fires me, too." She folded and handed over the paper. "Talking to you is better than reading a novel," she smiled. "And I want to know the next chapters. So promise you'll write?"

"I promise."

CHAPTER 12

Lucy felt strangely liberated when she bought her one-way ticket to Yuma the next morning. Even in the few months she'd worked in Los Angeles and rented a hotel room, she had accumulated more clothes and other small possessions than she now wanted to move. She'd left behind vases, picture frames, a small bookcase, and other odds and ends she'd gradually acquired. Traveling light with no more than she could stuff into one small valise was her goal.

As she settled into her window seat wearing a long gray skirt and matching jacket, she felt she was perhaps meant to be a wanderer or, to use a more acceptable term—a traveler. She wasn't meant for the settled life. For the one thing, she considered herself too young. She was still in her twenties and there was much of the world she had yet to see and experience.

The danger and adventure she'd already gone through, as Fran had noted, were more than most people experienced in a lifetime. But, it had only whetted her appetite for more. She had no great longing to see Marc Charvein; it was only a convenient reason to go to Yuma. There was no reason to think he or Sandoval would actually be there. Having no goals, no job, and no immediate prospects was unsettling. But, deep down, it was the thrill of the unknown she craved.

She'd read in the *Los Angeles Daily Times* of the series of robberies inflicted on the Southern Pacific trains in the past few months. Charvein had made only one brief visit a few weeks earlier when the train he was working as an express messenger made a forty-five minute meal stop at the Harvey House. She was worried about him later after she saw his name mentioned in a news article about a recent robbery where a dynamite blast had wrecked the express car. He'd been thoughtful enough—or maybe interested enough in her—to write and tell her he was unhurt. Her woman's intuition told her that a man of action like Charvein didn't write casual letters to friends unless there was some ulterior motive. True, what they'd been through together made them more than just casual friends. It was almost like two comrades who'd survived a war.

A bond had formed that would endure for a lifetime. Whatever his motivation for writing, he was still a friend and would remain so, even if their paths diverged for months at a time. She wondered if he would have written if she'd been married. She liked to think so, but then let that delicious speculation hang in the air as she raised the dusty window beside her seat. The fresh scent of sage and a whiff of locomotive wood smoke would help clear the city smell from her nostrils.

Marc Charvein was still her knight in shining armor, and he had fit that image when he showed up to rescue her from her abductors in Lodestar. She'd never gotten over her girlhood infatuation with medieval society. It had been her mental refuge from boredom. It was a world whose reality had been sanitized in her imagination. Even though mostly of her own creation, it was a world into which she'd been escaping for years—an era of history by which she still measured modern life.

Charvein and Sandoval led the horse, mule, and burro up a side ramp into an empty stock car. They pulled off the saddles and packs and piled them in a corner away from the soiled straw in the other stalls. Sandoval used a pitchfork to rake out the old manure and pile fresh straw in the three stalls, then forked a pile of clean straw into two more stalls to pad their bedrolls. Charvein scooped up a bucket of oats from a trough along the wall and gave each animal a bait of grain while Sandoval pumped two buckets of water from the well to one side of the rail yard. It would be enough to see the animals through to Gila Bend.

From his months spent prospecting alone in the Castle Dome mining district, Sandoval owned a well-worn pair of leather water bags that held about six gallons each and could be fastened together at the top and thrown across the withers of his pack mule, Lupida. In addition, each man carried on his saddle two blanket-sided half-gallon canteens—a total of one gallon per man. But, in that parched land where they were headed that would amount to no more than a day's supply per person, not counting what would be used for coffee and cooking. Water was heavy—just over eight pounds per gallon. So the burro was carrying right at 100 pounds of the life-saving liquid. They calculated it was enough to carry them from one spring or tank to another.

The freight rolled out to the chuffing of the mogul locomotive at 5:20 in the afternoon, right on schedule. The two men had been as unobtrusive as possible in their departure. As far as they were aware, only Coughlin, the dispatcher, and the train crew who helped them load up were aware of their destination at Gila Bend.

While the engine labored up the mountain grade just east of Yuma, Charvein was studying the map even closer. "I think we should go all the way to Tucson," he finally said. "Look here." He pointed and held the map for Sandoval to see. "We won't be that far east of San Felipe. And we're both familiar with the terrain south of there to the border. Should be plenty of water along the way."

Sandoval looked. Tucson was closer to the border than Gila

Bend, but it was farther east than they wanted to go. "Maybe split the difference and have the engineer let us off about here." He put a finger on a spot fifty miles northwest of Tucson. "Then, only the train crew will know where we are."

Charvein gave him a quizzical look. "Who would care?"

"Well, you never know." Sandoval paused in the act of thumbing tobacco into his pipe bowl. "I just have a feeling . . ." His voice trailed off. "No reason, really. But I have that same tickle at the base of my neck I had shortly before that bounty hunter, Breem Canto, jumped me."

"We'll decide when we get closer." Charvein folded up the map. "But you may be right. You and I have lasted this long because we were careful to watch our back trail and play our hunches. Wouldn't do to get careless now."

Sandoval took the precaution of smoking outside, away from all the flammable straw in the stock car. He retired through a small door at the end of the car to light up on the rear platform.

The train had reached the top of the grade and was picking up a little more speed, now exceeding twenty miles an hour as it began the descent toward the desert beyond.

The late spring heat had wilted Lucy's freshness of early morning. The orange ball of sun was nearly resting on the western horizon when the locomotive ground to a halt in a hiss of steam at the Yuma depot to discharge and pick up passengers and mail.

It had been a long, dusty ride from Los Angeles. Tired and stiff, she was ready to detrain, eat a good supper, and look for a hotel room. She'd made sure to trim the weight of her luggage to just what she could carry in one small valise. She'd learned her lesson by trying to lug a very heavy gold cross on long trips. Thank goodness that was over. She'd gone to the bank and closed her account, withdrawing her small savings in gold coin.

85

This amount she'd split up, carrying half of it in a leather coin purse, the other half stitched into the hem of her skirt. Experience had made her distrustful. The gold was in denominations no larger than quarter-eagles.

With both hands she wrestled her leather grip from the overhead rack, thinking she'd have to lighten it still further. Declining the offer of a porter to carry it, she lugged it down the steps, across the platform, and into the depot. The place looked and smelled just as she'd remembered it from that horrifying day months earlier when she, Charvein, and Sandoval had been accosted and captured at gunpoint by Stripe Morgan and forced to retrieve the gold cross from a depot locker. She shuddered at the recollection, then thrust it from her mind as she sat down on a bench in the waiting room. After a minute of collecting herself, she left the bag in plain sight and approached the barred ticket window. "Can you tell me where I might find Mister Marc Charvein?" she inquired.

The clerk frowned. "Who?"

"He's a Wells Fargo express messenger." She wondered why this man didn't know him.

The dispatcher in the next window overheard her and said, "He's out on a run, ma'am."

"East or west?"

The dispatcher looked at her without replying. "And what is your name?"

"Lucy Barkley. We're old friends. I haven't seen him in a few weeks."

"Oh, you're the one who was involved in all that excitement and shooting on a train awhile back." He motioned for her to come around the end of the partition. "Into my office."

She had a sudden qualm she was about to hear some bad news. What couldn't he tell her in the open? She retrieved her bag from the bench and followed him.

When the dispatcher had closed the door, he said, "How well do you know Charvein?"

"As well as I know anyone," she replied. "We saved each other's lives in Nevada."

"I had a hunch you were the one he spoke about." He took a deep breath. "He thinks a heap of you."

She could feel herself flushing.

The dispatcher took off his green eyeshade and tossed it on his desk. "Keep this to yourself, Miss Barkley, but he's on a mission to Mexico to see if he can get a lead on the gang that's been robbing the express cars."

Her stomach tightened. "Is he part of a posse?"

The dispatcher shook his head. "Our lawmen don't have jurisdiction south of the border. That's why he's doing this on the sly to see what he can find, if anything. Personally, I think it's a fool's errand, but nobody asked me. Dangerous, besides. The U.S. Cavalry crossed the border to chase Geronimo last year, but nothing was done about that. Guess the Mexican government didn't care. They were glad when the old war chief surrendered. Saved them the trouble. But he and his band are on the loose again. The Mex have been fightin' the Apache for years."

"So did he go alone?" She steered him back to her question.

"Just him and one other man who's new to Wells Fargo. Half-breed name of Carlos Sandoval."

She almost smiled. "I know him well. A very good man."

He nodded. "So that's about it. Can't tell you when they'll be back—or if," he added.

Her face must have shown worry because he continued, "Of course, I doubt they'll take any chances. As I understand it, this is just a scouting foray."

"Thanks for your information." She stood up. "When did they leave?"

"Loaded their animals and gear on a slow freight two hours ago. They'll get off at Gila Bend, he told me, and ride south."

"Thank you."

She gripped her leather bag and left the office. Pausing in the waiting room, she considered her next move. On a local freight, Charvein and Sandoval probably wouldn't reach Gila Bend until sometime tomorrow. Could she catch up? To what purpose? Then, she realized her urge for adventure was overwhelming her. She had a sudden desire to join them, and ride to Mexico. The three of them had been through a lot together. She no longer considered herself dependent on someone else to protect her. She'd taken the initiative and recruited a gambler and together they'd heisted the gold from the ruins of the church in Lodestar last year and escaped from under the nose of the mine owner. She and the gambler had made it all the way to the west coast. Then she'd slipped away from him with the gold cross and traveled up the Colorado River from the Sea of Cortez to Yuma. No longer was she the morning glory who shrank in the heat of the sun. She wasn't one of the medieval women of court she'd read about who were dependent on male protection.

But would Charvein and Sandoval allow her to join them? Not a chance, she admitted to herself. They'd either consider her a hindrance to fast travel, or they'd fear for her safety.

So, what to do? Send a telegraph message to Gila Bend that she was coming to join them? Yes. Not a request, but a statement. Yet, if they were forewarned, they'd ride off before her arrival.

She entered the open door of the adjacent Western Union office. Where was the telegrapher? Through the small, wavy panes of window glass she saw a man in shirtsleeves outside leaning against a porch post smoking a pipe. Probably waiting for a train, she thought. Wouldn't hurt to ask if he'd seen the telegrapher. She walked back into the depot and then out onto the platform. A few yards away, the stocky pipe smoker was engrossed in conversation with a slim, black-haired man seated on a keg. For some reason she couldn't explain, Lucy hesitated to approach. Maybe because they were talking quietly and glancing around every few seconds as if afraid of being overheard.

Carrying her grip, she peered down the track, pretending to watch for a train, then slouched back around a corner of the building. The low hum of conversation continued, and she slid up to the edge of the angled wall to see if she could eavesdrop. Apparently, an argument was developing. The auburn-haired man was waving his pipe around and urgently pressing a point. Voices were raised and she detected an Irish dialect. Nothing odd about that. Many Irishmen worked for the railroad. But suddenly she stiffened and listened more intently. The name "Charvein" caught her ear. A quick glance told her the black-haired man was growing irritated. He jumped up from the keg where he'd been sitting. "Why send any wire at all?" he grated in a rough voice. "It would just put 'em on their mettle."

"Odds are they'd never know," the stocky one answered. "But our lads must be alerted."

"Better let it be."

"B'God, I'll do my job or be damned," the stocky one blurted.

"Keep your voice down!" the lean man hissed, glancing around.

Lucy held her breath and flattened herself against the rough planks.

"Best not to go looking for trouble," the black-haired man continued. "This ain't the auld sod." He waved his arm toward the south. "There's miles and miles of waterless desert out there. Let that take care of those two. If they come back a'tall, they'll be worn to a frazzle. If anybody went lookin' for them, it'd be like trying to spot a coracle on the ocean."

"You can't be sure of that," the pipe smoker retorted. "What if they have a lead or two and get lucky?"

"Then send a wire to Mexico and warn them."

The stocky man shook his head. "You know damned well there're no telegraph wires anywhere close to them."

"Then let it go. No sense stirring the pot. We can rely on the land to discourage them. They'll just wander around for days or weeks, maybe get lost and die of thirst."

"I can't take that chance," the stocky man replied. "What the lads in Gila Bend do with the information is up to them, but they must be warned before Charvein and Sandoval have a chance to get wind of anything."

The black-haired man's pale complexion began to suffuse, and he turned away to apparently get his thoughts or emotions together. When he turned back, he said, "Then send the damned telegram to Gila Bend, but code it. What they do on the other end is up to them."

"I'll take care of it," the stocky man promised. "Then, if anything goes wrong, we're in the clear. If Face gets the word, he'll know how to handle it." He knocked the dottle out of his pipe on his boot heel, then blew through the stem to clear it. That ended the conversation, and he opened a narrow door and re-entered the Western Union office.

Lucy stepped back and exhaled the long breath she'd been holding. Her friends were in danger, but from whom or how, she couldn't determine. And who was this person referred to as Face? Her heart was pounding.

Now that she knew the telegrapher couldn't be trusted, she'd have to try to catch up to her friends on her own. Probably just as well they didn't know she was coming anyway. There was only one way to reach Gila Bend ahead of them. They were on a slow freight that would be sidetracked for any passenger express to be highballed through. If she could catch the next eastbound, she'd arrive ahead of them. If she'd only known this before she got off the train . . . but it had pulled out twenty minutes ago.

She walked quickly back into the depot and scanned the big chalkboard on the wall where arrivals, departures, and delays were constantly updated. She bit her lip when she saw the next eastbound passenger train wasn't scheduled to depart from Yuma for Gila Bend and Tucson until noon the next day. She'd never be able to head them off. What would happen as a result of the wire the Western Union man was probably tapping out right now?

Feeling tired and powerless, she sat down on a waiting room bench, placing her grip on the floor. Even if she somehow caught up with them, what would she warn them against? Someone connected with these robberies was obviously trying to stop them from scouting into Mexico. Other than that, she knew nothing. Apparently, this gang of robbers had spies everywhere—probably how they knew which trains to hit and which to leave alone.

What now? She looked up at the big wall map that depicted the route of the Southern Pacific. Where would they likely go after detraining at Gila Bend? She got up and approached the window where the dispatcher was working. "Pardon me, again," she said.

He looked up.

In a muted voice she asked, "Did Charvein and Sandoval say they would ride straight south from Gila Bend?"

"That was the plan."

She drew a deep breath. There were miles and miles of wilderness out there. The pair might go in any direction. There were only disconnected trails and seldom-used wagon roads. But . . . if she were to start now, this evening, she might intercept them. She was used to riding astride, and could toughen herself to days in the saddle. Going straight east, maybe she could head them off, or at least pick up the trail of where they'd stopped at any towns or mining camps. It was worth a try.

"Miss Barkley . . . ?"

"Huh? Yes?" She surfaced from her reverie to see the dispatcher staring at her.

"Was there anything else?"

"No . . . no, thank you. I'll just see them later." She turned away, her mind racing ahead. She walked quickly from the depot toward the livery two blocks away. The calm, rational side of her nature was whispering for her to forget this craziness, urging her to find a hotel and prepare to look for a job tomorrow. But the wild, reckless side of her was shouting at her to go, to ride out, to fling off caution and find Charvein. He was in some kind of danger and she was the only one who knew it, probably the only one who could warn him and Sandoval they were riding into a trap. Her imagination conjured up all kinds of terrible consequences from torture to sudden death.

When she looked up, she found her feet had already carried her to the rundown office of the livery stable. It was no contest; the reckless side of her nature had easily won out. She fumbled in the pocket of her skirt for the coin purse.

A realization slowly bubbled to the surface of her consciousness: she was in love with Marc Charvein, and had been for a long time.

Chapter 13

The train jolted to a halt, waking Charvein in the chill darkness. What now? There were no scheduled stops between Yuma and Gila Bend. Then he recalled they were on a freight and had probably been sidetracked for a passenger train.

He rolled to his feet, hearing their mounts shuffling in the nearby stalls. How far had they come? The stout mogul engine had been pulling their short freight over the mountains just east of Yuma when he went to sleep.

Exiting through the small door in the end of the stock car, he climbed down and looked up and down the train. The conductor was coming forward from the caboose, swinging his lantern.

"What's wrong?"

"A flare up ahead." The crewman moved past toward the locomotive.

Five minutes later he returned. "A washout. Might just as well tuck in for a nap. We'll be here a few hours until a work crew can get those timbers back in place."

Charvein sighed and climbed back inside.

"Why're we stopped?" Sandoval's voice came from the dark.

Charvein told him. "Go back to sleep. Nothing we can do to hurry it up."

The screech of brakes and a burst of steam woke Charvein and he cracked his eyes at daylight. Dust motes drifted through the shafts of afternoon sunlight slanting through the slatted sides of the stock car. GILA BEND announced a sign on the depot wall.

He'd slept soundly and felt rested, but felt odd to have slept away much of the day. Apparently, he was more fatigued than he thought—or was just relaxing once he was away from his boss.

"I'm hungry. What d'ya reckon they got to eat here?" He glanced over at Sandoval, who was sitting up a few yards away, brushing off the straw.

He tugged on his boots, and climbed stiffly to his feet, stretching. Sloshing some canteen water into his hand he scrubbed his face, then wiped on his sleeve. A few swallows cleared his dry throat.

"Sleep well?" Sandoval rose and shook out his blanket.

"Tolerably."

"We'd best get unloaded. How long is this stop?" Sandoval buckled on his gunbelt and reached for his hat. In the many months he'd spent camping in the desert, he'd acquired the habit of sleeping in his moccasins to protect his feet from any spines or insects.

"I'll find out." Charvein went out the small door at the forward end of the car and started forward to the locomotive.

"Need to unload the stock car. How long's the stop?" he yelled up at the engineer.

"We'll water up, and have a bite to eat," the lean man replied. He set the air brakes and swung down off the metal deck. "Forty minutes."

The brakeman and fireman, legs braced wide, walked atop the locomotive, swinging the counterbalanced spout of the water tank around, then pulled it down to fill the boiler.

"That'll give us time," Charvein said. He walked back to the stock car and peered between the slats at Sandoval. "Let's have some food before we unload. Last chance to eat somebody else's cooking for a while."

They went inside the café, and Charvein felt let down. He'd pictured something like a Harvey House, with its cleanliness, good service, and attractive, uniformed waitresses. As they sat down, he wondered if Lucy Barkley was still working at the Los Angeles Harvey House. He'd have to remember to stop and see her next time he made a run to the coast.

A balding man in a greasy apron waited on them. There wasn't much on the menu, but they ordered flapjacks with molasses along with ham and eggs to fortify themselves for the trail.

The only one already eating was the engineer. When the brakeman and fireman came in, Charvein and Sandoval were well into their food.

Ten minutes later, Charvein drained the last of his coffee. "Let's get unloaded while we have a little time." He rose and left a silver dollar on the table.

They strode out into the morning sunshine, Charvein felt full and satisfied as he inhaled a deep breath of the fresh desert air.

They went around the train and slid open the door to the stock car away from the depot platform. "Let's top off our canteens and water bag from that pump over there." Charvein settled the saddle in place on his mount and reached under for the straps.

Sandoval nodded, continuing to gather his gear. Both men's saddle scabbards carried Winchesters, drawn from Wells Fargo in Yuma. The holstered revolvers were their own personal weapons, and each man wore a full ammunition belt with extra shells in the saddlebags, just in case. For convenience, Charvein had made sure to requisition rifles that used the same .45 cartridges as their handguns.

Lacking a ramp, they jumped their animals down from the car.

Charvein reined his sorrel toward the rear of the train to pass around the caboose. The locomotive was closer, but his horse shied away from the panting black beast.

The two men dismounted at the shaded pump under a willow on the west side of the depot. Charvein worked the pump handle while Sandoval filled the pair of two-quart canteens each of them carried. The big leather water bag would come last.

"Taking the train all the way to Tucson would be a lot easier," Charvein remarked. "Only sixty miles to Nogales that way."

"Except that we'd have to ride miles out of our way after we crossed the border. You're getting soft, amigo."

"Reckon so."

Sandoval finished the canteens and hung them on the saddles. Then he dragged the partially limp leather bag from the cantle and pulled the cork stopper. As he held the mouth of the bag to the spout, Charvein began to pump.

The leather bag exploded in a shower of water at the same instant Charvein heard the boom of a big-bore rifle. He instinctively dove and rolled into the shelter of the depot platform a dozen feet away.

Sandoval jumped the other way and flung himself onto his mule, only a step ahead of a second shot that tore up the hard clay. Jeremiah lunged away, followed by Charvein's horse, which had been ground reined.

Charvein came to a crouch, gun in hand. The firing was from somewhere in the open land behind the depot. A cautious look around the edge of the platform showed him nothing but a gradual upslope of desert terrain. Except for a scattering of small creosote bushes, there was no cover. The shots had to have come from the low hills at least three-hundred yards away.

Sandoval rode to the other side of the train and reined up. The pack burro, Lupida, had bolted away thirty yards and stopped.

When no more shots came immediately, Charvein eased away from the platform and scrambled under a boxcar, joining Sandoval on the sheltered side.

"Where the hell did that come from?" His heart was thumping as he peered through the slats of the stock car.

"You see anything?"

"No. Too busy ducking," Charvein said. "Came from back yonder someplace. The only cover is those low hills a few hundred yards away." He studied the brush but saw no movement. And there was no sign of anyone in the more distant hills. A good marksman from that distance had come within a few inches of Sandoval, who was squatting down to fill the water bag.

The brakemen, engineer, and fireman had rushed outside, along with a waiter. "Who's shooting?" the brakemen shouted.

"Watch yourselves!" Charvein yelled from between the cars. "Somebody back behind the depot took a couple shots at us."

"What? Why?"

"Wish I knew. Here's where we leave you anyway." Charvein caught up his sorrel and mounted. "Let's go."

"Our water bag . . ." Sandoval hesitated.

"Forget it. There's a big hole in it that was meant for you. Let's ride!"

Their bedrolls, canteens, and rifles were on the saddles, so they pulled their mounts around and trotted away, Sandoval leading the burro, keeping the train between them and the sniper.

After a half-mile they slowed their animals to a walk

"If I didn't know better, I'd think that bounty hunter, Breem Canto, was still alive and after you," Charvein said, trying to dredge up any possible reason for the ambush.

"No chance of that. Canto's dead. I told you all about him stalking me. Had to finally shoot him in self-defense. But, yes, he tried to kill me from long range with a rifle."

"Apparently, someone knows where we're headed and tried to discourage us—permanently," Charvein said. "You have any enemies I don't know about? I think that shot was meant for you. I made a bigger target, standing up at that pump handle with my back to the shooter."

Sandoval slowly shook his head. "No one I can think of. Mine has been a solitary life, mostly, until we hooked up again last year."

"Lucky you were near enough to hear the gunfire when the Apaches had our stage stopped," Charvein said, recalling their close brush with death on that earlier occasion.

"Yeah, strange how things work out. If I'd minded my own business and stayed put that day, we wouldn't have met again."

"Just damned bad luck that Breem Canto was riding shot-gun."

Sandoval shrugged. "Things happen. Who would have expected him to be a bounty hunter in his spare time? And even more unlikely, he happened to recognize my face from a wanted poster. If you hadn't wounded him when he tried to arrest me, I'd likely be in jail somewhere right now—for accidentally kill-ing my own wife."

"Shoulda finished the job when I had him in my sights right then," Charvein said.

"And you might have hanged for murder," Sandoval said. "No—better the way things worked out. I know for a fact Canto is dead because I shot him at close range in that arroyo." He shifted in the saddle and tugged down his wide hat brim against the morning sun. "But Canto's past history. That drygulcher back there could be another bounty hunter, I guess," he went on. "Somebody who recognized me since I started working with you at Wells Fargo."

"Not much chance of that. He was too far away to see your

face, even with field glasses," Charvein said. "We'll just have to be on our guard."

They rode silently with their own thoughts for a few minutes.

"Who knew we were headed across the border to do some scouting?" Sandovol mused aloud.

"It was supposed to be just Coughlin and the dispatcher. But you know how secrets like that leak out. Why? You think it might have been somebody from Yuma?"

Sandoval nodded. "Might be. We don't know who's in this gang. They could have inside men working for the SP."

Charvein mulled this over. "Yeah, we could be walking into a lot more than we realize. Somebody trying to discourage us from poking around in Mexico." He twisted in his saddle and looked back. The dusty railroad town of Gila Bend had faded from sight beyond a slight rise in the desert.

"You think those shots were meant to kill us, or just scare us?" Sandoval asked.

"Whoever it was, I'd say it was meant to leave at least one of us dead and scare hell outta the one who survived. Somebody knows who we are and where we're going."

Sandoval nodded. "My thinking, too. That first shot didn't miss me more than six inches, and only because I moved a fraction to get a better grip on that heavy water bag. I'm afraid my luck at surviving ambushes is going to run out soon."

"We'll push straight south and see if we can cover forty miles today before we make camp."

"Papago Wells?"

"No," Charvein said. "I studied the map. It's too far east of us. We'll make for Ajo. There's water along the base of the mountains down that way."

By the time the sun had tucked in behind the distant desert mountains, they had ridden roughly thirty miles. "Let's pick a good spot and camp while it's still light," Sandoval suggested.

"Fine with me. My rear end could use a rest. I haven't ridden any distance for a good while."

They made camp at the base of a small hill that concealed their campfire from the west. Watering the horse, mule, and burro out of their hats, they picketed the animals near a small amount of grass and a clump of mesquite. Each of the men took turns standing watch.

When the rosy eastern sky made it just light enough to see, they cooked up bacon and coffee and chewed on some hard bread. They'd been in their saddles a half-hour by the time early rays of sun were lancing across the desert floor.

Charvein watched their back trail but there was no sign of anyone. Nothing but dun-colored desert and a scattering of creosote bush and mesquite in every direction. A series of shallow, dry washes angled southeast to northwest along their route. No sign of any roads or trails. They rode in a wide, shallow valley with the jagged line of the Sand Tank Mountains to the east and the Sauceda Mountains to the west and south.

"We'll make Ajo well before sunset," Charvein said. "I haven't been to this part of the territory before, but the map I studied is supposed to be pretty accurate."

"You think that rifleman could have gotten ahead of us?" Sandoval wondered.

"If he'd been willing to ride a lot harder and a lot farther than we did, I guess so," Charvein said, his nerves edgy in spite of having had several hours of exhausted sleep the night before.

"If we knew how desperate he was to gun us down, maybe we could figure out what lengths he'd go to," Sandoval said.

CHAPTER 14

"Probably another ten miles or so to Ajo," Charvein remarked late in the afternoon.

"Is it a town?" Sandoval asked. "What's there?"

"Two years ago, nothing," Charvein said. "There'd been a mining operation, but it was abandoned. A friend of mine who was down this way a few months ago said a couple of men have started up the mine again. But it's the closest thing we'll see to civilization until we get across into Mexico."

Sandoval suddenly reined up.

"What's wrong?" Charvein was startled.

"Thought I saw something move over that rise." He nodded toward their right front. "Gone now."

Charvein's throat constricted, and he unlimbered his Winchester from its sheath.

"I wonder if our bushwhacker somehow got ahead of us?"

"Just caught a glimpse," Sandoval said, kneeing his horse to a walk. "Could've been anything. Even a javelina."

"They generally travel in packs."

"In case it was human, let's bear a bit to the left, down into that dry wash," Sandoval said. "I'd feel a lot safer if the lighting wasn't so good—maybe at dusk or dawn."

But it was neither.

Charvein uncased his field glasses and scanned the low rise two-hundred yards ahead. He saw nothing out of the ordinary.

"Just be ready for anything," he said, softly, putting away the glasses.

They bore down into the dry wash and immediately Charvein had a trapped feeling when he couldn't see a good distance in every direction. *Just nerves,* he thought. But his eyes and ears were tuned to sense the slightest sound or movement. He looked up. High overhead a hawk was soaring on the rising thermals. Their mounts' hooves were kicking up the dry, cracked mud in the bottom of the wash, raising a fine cloud of dust that could probably be seen for some distance. But nothing could be done about it.

A quarter mile later they came up out of the declivity. There was nothing in sight and they rode silently along, scanning the desert terrain in all directions. The peaceful landscape dozed in the warm spring sunshine. After another hour of slow riding, the brown range of hills visible in the clear air looked barely closer than before

Charvein pointed. A green line of willows and cottonwoods angled across their path, a half-mile ahead.

"Water?"

"Yeah. Probably the stream that flows near Ajo. No wells or springs hereabouts that I know of. So the Indians have to use it, too."

Charvein still held his Winchester across the saddle.

They were less than 200 yards from the stream when a horseman emerged from the tree line. Charvein caught a glimpse of long black hair flying before the horse and rider disappeared into a swale.

Both men drew rein and slid from their saddles, Charvein looking quickly for cover. Nothing offered but a thick clump of mesquite. Holding his horse with one hand, he jerked his head in that direction. "Here!"

They looped the reins to the largest branch and went to their knees in the soft soil, Sandoval with his Colt in hand. Charvein's heart pounded and his mouth was dry. They waited.

A minute later the rider galloped into view, and Charvein jacked a round into the chamber. He leveled his rifle. The lone Apache's black hair was flying in the wind. Then the warrior disappeared, momentarily obscured by brush. *Apaches don't usually travel alone,* he thought. *Maybe some scout sent to draw us out so we can be cut down.*

The rider came into view again fifty yards distant and Charvein's finger tightened on the trigger.

Suddenly, Sandoval's hand slammed down on the barrel and the rifle exploded, the slug plowing up dirt ten feet away.

"*What . . . ?*"

"No, señor! It's a woman."

They scrambled out of the mesquite for a better look as she approached. A familiar face and form . . .

She slid her horse to a stop and leapt from the saddle.

"Marc!"

"Lucy!" Charvein was shocked. "By God."

She sprang to him, locking her arms around his neck as they embraced. Her hair smelled of dust and wood smoke. She was even slimmer than he remembered. Startled, he could think of nothing to say. Finally, he pushed back and held her at arm's length. "What the hell are you doing here so . . . ?" She was flushed and wind-burned and—he was suddenly aware—very pretty. Her hat hung by its cord on her back and her long black hair was loose.

She only smiled, apparently enjoying the moment. "I came looking for you."

"Out here?"

"Let's get to the shelter of the trees by the river and I'll tell you all about it." She stepped over and kissed Sandoval on his lean, beardless cheek. "My two best friends. What a relief to see you!"

She gathered up the reins of her horse and mounted. Charvein and Sandoval followed her lead. Charvein shoved his rifle into its scabbard.

"I spotted some Apaches a good ways off earlier today," she said as they held their horses to a walk. "But I hid down in some thick willows, praying they weren't coming to the river. They did, but they were around the bend a couple hundred yards from where I was." She patted the holstered revolver. "I carried this, but doubt it would have been much good had they spotted me," she continued. "Thank God, they didn't, and I was downwind. I managed to keep my horse quiet," she said. "At first I thought you were two more renegades. Couldn't tell from a distance, but I did remember to bring these." She held up her field glasses.

As they rode and talked, Charvein's eyes were constantly roving about, watching their back trail and probing every uneven place in the desert where a man or horse could be concealed. His vigilance had become almost as automatic as breathing.

It was some time past four, Charvein estimated by the sun, when they reached the line of cottonwoods and dismounted. They let their four animals plunge their muzzles into the clear stream that gurgled over the rocks and a long gravel bar.

"Give us the story." Charvein took his two canteens and squatted by the water's edge to submerge them.

She took a long drink from her canteen before she answered. "Dry out here," she commented. "It's been a long, hard chase trying to cut you off."

"You knew where we were?" Charvein asked.

"More or less. At least I hoped to pick up your trail."

"Start at the beginning." Refreshing as it was to see her, Charvein feared her presence would complicate their search.

She told the story of her job and how it ended, and of the good friend who'd stood by her in the crisis.

Charvein was glad to hear she had at least one female friend. She'd never spoken of others before. He'd always had the feeling she was more at home in the company of men.

"So I came back to Yuma hoping you might be around. I needed some straight advice from an old friend. Didn't want to be a waitress all my life, anyway. I have to decide what to do next." She smiled at Sandoval. "It's great to have both of you here."

"How did you know where we were?"

"The dispatcher said you'd gone off on some special assignment." She gently rubbed her sunburned nose. "Told me you were scouting across the border for some train robbers. Didn't know if or when you'd be back." She shrugged. "Sounded like he thought it was a wasted trip." She went on to relate her chance overhearing of the strange conversation between the telegrapher and another Irishman. "They knew where you'd gone and were apparently planning some mean surprise. I couldn't let that happen. But there were no trains eastbound that would be able to catch you, and I couldn't use the telegraph without them knowing. So . . ." She shrugged. "Here I am. It was a long shot."

Sandoval and Charvein exchanged glances.

"I thank you for that," Charvein said. "But someone tried to get us at Gila Bend." And he described their brush with death the previous afternoon.

"The dispatcher said, to save the horses, you were taking the train as far as Gila Bend and then would ride south. I took a good look at a map and inquired at the livery about waterholes and villages and mines on that route. Bought two horses and gear and decided to head you off. Figured from the time you left I might be able to cut your trail somewhere near Ajo."

"You must have been riding hard," Sandoval said. "Terrible desert between here and Yuma."

"Yes," she nodded. "I wouldn't attempt it in summer. Never saw an Indian, or even a single human until I got near here. Wore out my horse and turned him loose, then switched to my spare. Stashed my extra gear near a spring. Somebody might find it and use it."

"You still wouldn't have headed us off, if the train hadn't been delayed most of a day by a washout in one of those bridged arroyos," Sandoval said.

"You might have died." Charvein looked at her lean figure, her sunburned skin, appreciating even more what she'd endured in an effort to warn them.

"No, *you two* might have died," she responded. "I knew that telegrapher was alerting someone in Gila Bend, but I didn't know that's where they'd try to ambush you. I was hoping maybe someone there would just pick up your trail and follow. These people must be really desperate."

Charvein hung his canteens back on the saddle horn. "Let's ride," he said.

"I was hoping maybe we could camp soon," she said. "I'm exhausted."

"We'll camp, but not near the river. Ajo is just a few miles farther. We'll find a good spot before we get there."

The three swung into their saddles and splashed the animals across the shallow stream.

"Too much cover here," Sandoval explained. "Even with one of us standing guard, some Apache or white might be able to sneak up on us. Lupida is a good lookout and would bray a warning, but no sense in chancing it."

"That's right," Charvein said. "There should be a better site a couple miles from these trees."

A dry desert wash provided a campsite just as the sun disappeared in a wash of gold and red behind the desert hills. They gathered brush and small dead driftwood left from some previous flash flood and built a small campfire to make coffee and heat up beans laced with strips of jerky.

Charvein knelt on his ground cover and sipped the scalding coffee, feeling his flagging energy begin to revive. Dusk was settling in, but the cheerful small fire threw light on their faces.

Lucy sat on a blanket, eating and drinking the coffee.

"You look all in," Charvein said, still wondering at her efforts to save them.

She nodded. "I'll admit I'm limp as a saddle blanket. Just the letdown of finding you, I guess. The search and the effort were what kept me going until now."

"Don't worry. You can sleep as long as you like tonight."

"That'll be nice. I haven't slept very soundly lately. Never realized how lonely the desert can be at night. Strange critters out hunting each other. The sounds I can't hear are what frighten me most. It's a comfort to have you two here standing guard."

"We'll take turn about on watch." Sandoval got up and poured himself another cup of coffee from the blackened pot setting on a flat rock beside the small blaze. "I'll volunteer to take it first until midnight as long as I'm wide awake."

Charvein finished eating, poured a tiny bit of water into his tin plate, and scoured it out with sand before stashing it in his saddlebags on the ground. "So, bring us up to date on your life since we saw you last." He leaned back on his saddle, holding a full cup.

"There's really not much to tell," Lucy said. "Mostly just working as a waitress at the Harvey House." She went on to tell them about the strange man who had tried to become familiar with her. "He thought he could get away with it, because apparently he's rich and powerful," she said. "But I never heard of him. Just some greasy-looking, arrogant customer."

"What was his name?" Charvein asked.

She frowned. "Something odd. Let me think." She hesitated. "It sounded foreign. Ad . . . Adolph Grindell, that's it!"

"Adolphus Grindell," Charvein repeated, looking at Sandoval.

Sandoval shook his head. "Well, now we know a bit more about this man."

"You know him?" Lucy asked.

"Not really. We know *of* him. We tried to look him up at his office in Los Angeles recently, but he wasn't there, or that's what we were told, even though we were posing as customers— not Wells Fargo agents, so as not to put him on his guard," Charvein said.

"What in the world did you want with him?"

"He ships a lot of gold jewelry by Wells Fargo and much of it has been stolen when the express cars were robbed the past few months."

"We thought to question him about these shipments. It wouldn't be the first time a shipper was in collusion with the robbers. The shipper collects the reimbursement from Wells Fargo for the stolen goods and then splits with the robbers. Everyone but our company comes out ahead."

"But you didn't see him?" she asked.

"That's right. We were told he was out of town." Charvein shrugged. "We thought with some indirect questioning, to get a feel for this man. Sometimes you can tell a good deal more about a man by how he acts and his manner as by what he actually says."

"Well, I can tell you how he acts around me." She compressed her lips at the recollection.

"Business is business," Sandoval said. "Apparently, he's the type who considers women as recreation. That's the way that damned deputy marshal treated my wife when she was waiting tables."

His hooded eyes narrowed and he spat to one side. Both Charvein and Lucy knew not to bring up anything more about this story of Buck Rankin. Lucy had shot him, almost two years earlier. Apparently the memory of the late marshal was still bitter in Sandoval's mind.

"That's an odd connection," Charvein mused. "But maybe Grindell has nothing to do with these robberies. That's what we hope to find out. One thing we do know—somebody doesn't want us to go poking around down in Mexico."

Charvein started to ask Lucy if she intended to ride along with them. But he thought better of it. Let the question simmer until morning when all of them were rested and not looking at the world through the lens of fatigue and stress. He already knew the answer, anyway. He had to offer to let her accompany them. After what she'd endured to warn them, he couldn't very well send her on her way alone. If she wanted to stay with them, in spite of any potential danger, he must let her stay. It was her choice. And he knew from recent history she could stand up to anything he could. She wouldn't flinch. Lucy Barkley was a much more mature person than she'd been when he first rescued her from the hostage-taking convicts in Lodestar many months earlier. *God! That seemed like ages ago.*

"This fire can't be seen down in the swale of the desert," Charvein said. "But we'll let it die down anyway." He got up and stretched his tired muscles. "Probably ought to take an extra cup of coffee with you on watch," he said to Sandoval. "Can't afford to get sleepy."

"Already got it." The lean, dark man hefted his rifle in one hand, and padded away to climb the slope several yards away. He stretched out beneath a screening creosote bush, facing north. The binoculars were looped around his neck on a strap.

Lucy spread her blanket near the glowing coals of the fire as the night air grew chilly. She approached Charvein and touched his arm. "Thank you," she said, simply.

"What for? I should be thanking you for trying to alert us." He wanted to take her in his arms, but thought this maybe wasn't the time. He squeezed her hand briefly, then sank down onto his own bedroll on the sand.

He was asleep within minutes.

It seemed he'd barely closed his eyes when Sandoval roused him to go on sentry duty.

He sat up, groaning with fatigue and stiffness. He reached for his boots and gunbelt.

"Everything quiet," Sandoval reported.

"What time is it?"

"Between one and two I'd guess." He handed over the rifle and the field glasses. "Moonset soon."

"Okay." Charvein took the weapon and the binoculars and climbed the slope to investigate their back trail from the screen of bushes.

Before the moonlight faded, he carefully moved in a wide circle around their camp, stepping softly and carefully to avoid any spiny cacti or rocks. All seemed quiet and secure. When he completed the circuit, he was wide awake, but still very tired. His body craved more rest.

Twenty years ago, lack of sleep and sore muscles wouldn't have bothered me, he thought, settling under the creosote bush. He pushed the thought aside and used the field glasses to scan a complete circle, section by section, studying every plant, watching for any sign of movement. Once he saw a tiny motion, but after intense scrutiny, decided it was some small mammal. He felt sure he was not scouting for Apaches, since they would never be seen if they didn't want to. And, to his knowledge, Apaches usually attacked just before dawn when their victims would be most vulnerable with fatigue.

He felt sure, from what Lucy had said about the telegram from Yuma to Gila Bend, that their assailants had been white. If those who'd ambushed them were serious and persistent, they'd be the ones to look out for. Perhaps those shots had only been a one-time effort to kill or discourage him and Sandoval from heading for Mexico. Maybe the gunmen were not following after all. But Lucy had told them the telegrapher, Dugan, had said he couldn't send a telegraph message to Mexico because there was not a telegraph wire anywhere close. Close to what? Whoever Dugan was protecting. So it was more than likely the shooters from Gila Bend were on their trail. In any case, he and Sandoval dared not let down their vigilance.

CHAPTER 15

Their stop at the Ajo mine the following day was brief. When they rode up just before noon, a guard with a rifle blocked their way.

"Who are you and whatta ya want?" the bearded, ragged man demanded.

"Just water and maybe buy a little grub from you," Charvein replied. He could see the shored-up entrance to a tunnel in the hillside fifty yards beyond.

"Crick's over yonder about a half-mile." He jerked his head in the general direction. "As to grub, we ain't got any to spare. Barely enough to feed ourselves."

Charvein saw no signs of a settlement anywhere about.

As if reading his mind, the guard said, "Iffen we don't kill some meat close by, we hafta haul everything from a good many miles away."

At that moment, another man emerged from the tunnel pushing a wheelbarrow and dumped a load of spoil down the slope. He paused and stared at them but made no move to approach.

"You see anyone come by here in the last day or so?" Sandoval asked.

"Nope. Just you three."

Charvein sat his horse, leaning forward on the saddle horn. A long silence ensued.

"We gotta mine to run here," the guard finally said. "You'd best be movin' on."

"Obliged," Charvein nodded, pulling his horse's head around.

The three rode away toward the line of trees that marked the water.

"Not too neighborly," Lucy remarked when they were out of earshot.

"Reckon they're just being cautious with strangers," Charvein said. "Looks like a two-man operation. If trouble comes, they have to be ready."

"This is a very old mine location," Sandoval said. "Spanish priests and Indians first worked it sometime in the 1770s. Then, the story goes, they were run off and many of them killed by the Apaches, and no one dared come back here until the past few years."

"The gold must be rich, if those two men are risking their lives," Lucy said.

"Except for a few renegades, the Apaches are mostly on the run now," Sandoval said. "And it's not so much gold as copper and silver that's found hereabouts."

They got down in the shade of the small gravelly stream, let the horses drink their fill, and then loosened the girths to allow them to graze on the nearby grass. The men refilled all the canteens. Charvein again regretted the big water bag being shot to a useless piece of leather.

Sandoval spread a map on the rough bark of a fallen cotton-wood.

"How far to the next water?" Charvein asked.

Sandoval shook his head. "Maybe a day's ride. Sonoita Creek. After that, it's only a few miles to the border, and then . . . who knows? It shows the creek flows all the way south along the eastern edge of the Gran Desierto to the gulf. But it could be dry before it gets that far south. Still, we've had a decent amount of rain this spring . . ."

"But it's getting on to the dry season," Charvein said.

Lucy stood looking from one to the other, apparently depending on their experience and judgment to make the right decision. "Where is this village you told me you're looking for?" she asked.

"Doctor Vance marked it right here." Sandoval pointed to a penciled *X* just south of the international boundary and slightly to the east of Sonoita Creek.

"That's about sixty miles, I'd guess," she said. "Two days, maybe? Why isn't it printed on the map?"

"This is only a map of the territory," Charvein said. "And not a very good one, at that. But it was the best one I could find without waiting weeks to order one from Washington."

Sandoval shrugged and began folding the map. "We should be able to find it. A lot of rough mountains between here and the border. Our water should last if we go easy on it. Maybe by following the low valleys and canyons we'll find a sink or a spring. Once we hit the village, there has to be a source of water, even if it's wells, or the people couldn't live there."

After a thirty-minute rest they mounted up and rode out, heading as nearly straight south as the terrain would allow.

That night they camped at the base of a low desert mountain, their small campfire shielded by several huge boulders that had been dislodged over time from a higher ledge. A seep of water emerged from the base of the hill and created several square yards of marshy ground grown up with reeds. It supplied the animals with all they wanted to drink.

The next day they again rode south. By midafternoon, Sandoval, by consulting the map and gazing around at the formation of the hills, guessed they had crossed the border, but there was nothing to mark the artificial boundary in this remote location.

Two miles farther on they reined up when they intersected a dirt road running generally east and west across their path.

"This must be the Mexican equivalent of El Camino del Diablo," Charvein said. "It's supposed to parallel the border across the desert just like the road on the American side."

"Then San Felipe must be only a short few miles east." Sandoval again consulted the map he pulled out of his saddlebag.

They turned their mounts and rode on, the westering sun now at their backs. Two miles farther on, they came across a peasant and a cart drawn by a donkey. They were resting in the shade of a hillside. The man, who was smoking a pipe, leapt up when he saw them and reached for something in his wooden cart.

"*Hola!*" Sandoval held up his hand. "*Amigo.*"

The Mexican hesitated, but didn't take his hand from under a bundle in the cart.

"Probably holding a rifle," Charvein muttered under his breath. "Be careful."

Staying on the road, they walked their horses within twenty yards of the man, indicating their peaceful intentions by holding their hands in plain sight.

"*Donde esta San Felipe?*" Sandoval inquired politely.

"*Dos horas.*" The peasant pointed east along the road they were traveling.

"*Gracias.*"

The trio rode on without stopping.

"Good. Easier than I thought," Charvein said when they were a hundred yards beyond the peasant.

The sun was casting long, moving shadows ahead of them when the low adobe buildings appeared like square lumps of brown sugar a half-mile ahead.

Maybe a settlement of five hundred or so, Charvein guessed. But dirt poor, he noted when they got close enough to see details clearly by the last rays of the slanting sunlight. Riding slowly down the main street, their horses scuffing up puffs of dust, they drew curious stares, as strangers always did in a place so isolated. Several men, sporting black mustaches and wearing rough work clothes, lounged on the wooden porch of the cantina, drinks in hand, several smoking cigarillos. The light evening breeze brought the smell of strong tobacco to Charvein's nose. He had a prickly feeling up his back, but pretended to only casually glance their way as the trio rode past.

"Ask one of them where the Fortuna family lives," Charvein said *sotto voce* to Sandoval.

Carlos nodded and pulled up at the open-air blacksmith shop where the muscular, hairy smith was just pulling off his leather apron. A young boy was putting away the tools.

"Pardon," Sandoval began, and then in Spanish pleasantly inquired for the family they were seeking.

The boy looked at the smith as if asking permission to answer.

The big blacksmith was one of the mightiest men Charvein had ever seen. He wore a sleeveless undershirt revealing bulging biceps, hairy forearms and chest, and a dark, week-old growth of beard under a drooping mustache the size and thickness of a black cat's tail. He had black eyebrows to match, but the hair on top of his head was thinning.

He replied in rapid, harsh-sounding Spanish—more of a bark than a reply.

Sandoval said something in a calm tone, gesturing, and Charvein caught the name of Doctor Vance.

The blacksmith replied briefly, pointing up the street the way they were headed. His suspicious gaze slid toward Lucy, who kept her eyes averted.

"Gracias," Sandoval said and kneed his horse forward. "Let's go," he said softly. "The *hombre* the doc treated lives down here on the corner."

They rode silently for a minute.

Charvein tried to quickly plan his strategy. They were mostly just feeling their way along here in a strange village in a foreign country. He was glad for Sandoval's knowledge of Spanish to gain access to these people. But what would they say they'd come looking for? He had a vague notion the strange, handmade gold coin Doc Vance had showed them had something to do with the train robberies. But what? Maybe it would begin to come clear if they questioned the family. It might be difficult to gain their confidence. Even though he feared for her safety, Charvein was now grateful for Lucy's presence, since he sensed the villagers, always suspicious of strangers and fearful of *bandidos,* would be less wary if a white woman was riding with them.

"Which one of these houses did he say the Fortunas lived in?" Charvein asked.

"I'm not sure," Sandoval said, "and I didn't want to press him for details. He wasn't inclined to be friendly."

"I can show you, señor."

Charvein was startled by the voice that came from the shadows between two adobes only a few yards away. He strained to see, and then recognized the boy who'd been helping the blacksmith.

"You speak English."

"*Sí.* Follow me." The boy slipped out of the shadows and jogged along the dusty street without looking back.

They walked their tired horses, Sandoval leading the burro, and casually followed the boy.

It was the supper hour and the street was mostly deserted. The smoke of cooking fires drifted from several chimneys. Only a couple of men, lounging on the porch of a mercantile, stared curiously as they rode slowly past.

At the end of the short block, the boy turned into a cross street. As they reined their mounts off the main street, the boy motioned for them to come ahead.

The three dismounted and let their animals drink from a stone water trough.

"*La casa de la Fortuna.*" He indicated the adobe behind him. "I am a friend of the Fortuna family. I am a friend of Doctor Vance."

"You're the one who brought the doc when Juan Fortuna was wounded?"

"*Sí.* The doctor lives only a few miles that way." He pointed northeast toward the border. "You wish to see Juan and his wife, Consuela?"

"Yes."

"My name is Diego," he said. "I will fetch them for you."

He knocked on the doorframe, then ducked inside. The door itself stood open to the evening air.

Charvein heard some indistinct conversation in Spanish inside. Then a sharp few words, but the voices became softer.

When he'd begun to think no one was coming out, a woman in a faded cotton dress appeared in the doorway. Diego was behind her.

"This is Consuela Fortuna," the boy said to Charvein.

Sandoval greeted her in Spanish.

She replied, her eyes wary, taking in Lucy, who stood in the middle.

Then Sandoval began to question the woman, his voice gentle. He paused when she answered.

"I asked for her husband because it's customary for the man to deal with strangers or take care of business," Sandoval said. "She apologized for not inviting us inside for a cool drink, but her husband, Juan, is asleep just now. He is still recovering from a gunshot wound he suffered from bandits."

"Tell her we will relay the good news of his healing to Doctor Vance," Charvein said.

Sandoval translated.

Instead of excusing himself and departing as Charvein expected, Diego stood there, looking from one to another, listening. Charvein wondered if he was waiting for a tip, but then decided the boy considered himself an interested bilingual spokesman for this family, if not for the entire village. The dingy cotton shirt and short pants hung on his bony frame. Homemade sandals protected his feet.

"Tell her Doctor Vance said some bandits tried to steal their gold," Charvein said. Then, under his breath so only Sandoval could hear, "We must be very cautious about this, so she knows there is nothing to fear from us."

Sandoval paused and then began to speak in Spanish. Charvein wished he could understand the words. But his manner and voice seemed gentle and persuasive.

"Should I ask her where she and her husband got the gold coin?" Sandoval looked at Charvein.

"I can tell you!" Diego suddenly interrupted.

They all looked at him.

"I would not say if you were not friends of Doctor Vance," the boy continued. "But he is honest and heals many in the village without pay."

This young teen acted and talked almost like an adult. Charvein guessed the lad had probably been forced to grow up quicker to cope with his hard life here.

The doctor had already related the story about the Fortunas receiving the coin from some mysterious nightrider, but Charvein wanted to hear the details directly from the woman herself. How much truth was in such a tale? He wanted to study her face as she related the story and, if possible, ask a question or two.

Sandoval said something in Spanish to Consuela.

She did not reply. Finally, after several long seconds, she gave a short response.

"She does not wish to speak of it," Sandoval said.

"If you buy me a beer, I will tell you," Diego said quietly to Charvein.

"*Gracias, señora.*" Charvein turned to Sandoval. "Apologize for us disturbing her."

Sandoval said something in Spanish and replaced his hat as he mounted his mule.

"*De nada.*" The gray-haired woman replied and turned to re-enter the house.

"There is a cantina nearby," Diego said when she was gone. "They have good *cerveza* and I know a place where we can talk so no one can hear."

An hour later, just after full dark, a gigantic full moon cast a bright orange light through the haze just above the horizon.

The three travelers and the boy sat on flat rocks near the edge of a gravelly stream that coursed along the outskirts of the village.

Diego hurriedly snatched up some dry brush to add to the few dry sticks of driftwood Sandoval had piled on the rocky shore, and Charvein kindled a small fire. It was for light and warmth against the evening chill since they had nothing to cook, not even coffee.

Charvein had bought tortillas stuffed with frijoles and peppers for all of them, along with a big growler of beer they shared in their tin cups.

Diego sat cross-legged and tore into his food as if he hadn't eaten in two days. At his age and from the looks of his bony frame, Charvein guessed it would take a lot of food to fuel that growing body—food he apparently didn't get enough of.

They ate silently, savoring the spicy food. The moon slowly lost its orange glow as it climbed higher above the horizon.

Diego finished eating before the rest, and wiped his fingers in the soft white sand. Then he held out his cup for a refill and Sandoval obliged, topping it off with the foamy brew.

"You are in luck if you wish to know who brings the gold to our village." The boy wiped his mouth with the back of his hand.

He leaned back from the circle of firelight and looked into the darkness beyond.

They waited in silence for more.

He turned back, leaning in toward the fire and lowered his voice. "Because the horseman in black rides only when the moon is full, as it is tonight. Every month since last year he has come."

"Tonight?" Sandoval asked.

"*Sí.* Or tomorrow night. I cannot tell when the moon is really full."

"Nobody knows who this rider is or where he comes from?" Charvein asked.

"No."

"Does he always ride alone?"

"*Sí.*"

"Are the Fortunas the only ones who receive these coins?"

"Oh, no. Those who are poorest."

"How are they chosen?"

"I do not know. The Fortunas have received three of the coins since Christmas."

"Does this mysterious rider visit other villages as well?" Lucy asked.

"*Creo que sí.*" He pointed over his shoulder toward the west. "A priest who visits our village told of a family in Sonoita who received such a coin last month."

Charvein looked at Sandoval and Lucy. "There must be more than one rider if he visits several villages the same time each month."

"Almost like Saint Nick whose sled must fly to all parts of the world in the one night," Lucy chuckled.

"This is not a story for jokes." Diego sounded offended. "News of this has spread, and *bandidos* have heard of it. Never before had they bothered our village, but now they are drawn by this gold. They will steal or kill to get what they want. Juan Fortuna is the father of my good friend. He is lucky to be alive. He would not tell the *bandidos* where his gold was."

"I'm sorry," Lucy said. "I didn't mean to sound flippant."

Diego looked puzzled. "I don't know this . . . 'flippant.' "

She shook her head. "Never mind. I know this is serious."

"It is not always the same night, but only *around* the time of the full moon—within a few days."

"Do the masked riders leave the gold only with those who are very poor?" Sandoval poked up the fire that was dying down to coals.

"No. The priest said the gold is given to those who have big trouble. The daughter of a *familia* he knows was lost in a bad flood. Her *familia* received a gold coin. They were not poor. Her *padre* was a saddle maker."

They were silent for a minute. Charvein rubbed his tired eyes and shifted away from the smoke of the fire. What in the world could these strange gifts of gold mean? What was the purpose? And did it really have any connection to the robberies of the Southern Pacific trains? He looked at Diego, who was finishing the beer in his cup.

"Do you know if anyone has tried to find out who this rider—or these riders—are?" Charvein asked.

"Many *hombres* meet in the cantina to talk. They will not make this rider stop. The *alcalde* said to stop this *caballero* would be like to dig up a spring. It could stop the flow of water."

"A wise man," Sandoval murmured. "Do the *Federales* know about this?"

"I do not know," the boy answered. "The soldiers have not come here in a long time. But at least some *bandidos* know."

"Was anyone else in San Felipe injured or killed by these outlaws?"

"No. The Gonzales family was robbed, but no one was shot because they gave up their gold coin."

Another pause in the conversation while they finished their food and poured the last of the beer into their cups. Charvein wondered, if the robbers knew how the gold was being distributed, why they didn't waylay the mysterious riders who were doling it out, instead of attacking the villagers. He voiced his question aloud to the group.

"Perhaps these masked riders are armed, while the villagers make an easier target," Sandoval said. "In my experience, those who rob and injure the poor and defenseless are not overly brave."

"And if these riders are expected, do the villagers wait up to see them?" Lucy asked.

"Some hide in the shadows and watch for them." Diego stood up and stretched. The flickering firelight emphasized the hollows under his eyes and made him look older than his years. "I have seen the rider once myself."

They leaned forward to hear his description. "All I saw was a dark shape on a fast horse. He wore a hat and a mask and a black *capa*."

"A cape?"

"It was cold that night. He did not dismount. I saw him ride up to a house and drop something on the doorstep. Then he rode to the end of the village, and dropped another coin at *la casa* where an *hombre* has the coughing sickness."

"Sounds as if he knew exactly where he was going," Lucy said. "Nothing haphazard about it."

"*Sí.*"

"The rider never leaves a message?" Lucy wondered.

"No. Just the coin wrapped in a small package."

Charvein rose. "Diego, take this empty growler back to the cantina, *por favor.*" He was very tired, but nervous energy would keep him going this bright, moonlit night. "We'll camp near this stream. Do you think the nightrider will come near midnight?"

The boy shrugged. "*¿Quien sabe?*" he replied. "I will stay up late and watch, and many others will as well." He grinned. "It has become like a quiet fiesta. Many men bring cigars and *cerveza* and stay up until after midnight to watch. But they are careful and do not show themselves. The nights of the full moon are an exciting time in San Felipe." He took the beer container and started away. "Will you also be watching?" he asked.

"I think we just might," Charvein said.

The boy moved away. Charvein watched him go, and then turned to Sandoval. "We have to stay awake," he said, even though he felt himself sinking with accumulated fatigue.

"I'll keep watch." Sandoval grinned. "I'm younger and stronger."

Charvein let the jibe pass, knowing it was probably true.

"But what is the plan if we see him?" Sandoval continued. "Try to stop him, question him? He could put up a fight and start shooting if he thinks we're bandits."

Charvein tried to force his tired brain to think, to come up with some scheme. "There will be villagers watching, so we must wait until he passes on out of town."

Lucy shook her head. "Our animals are tired. He'll be on a strong, fast horse. If he gets beyond the village, we'll never catch him."

"If we try to stop him when he slows down, the villagers will give us much trouble," Sandoval said.

"So we have to jump him from ambush right after he makes his drop and starts away."

"You never did explain why you want him," Lucy said.

"I have a hunch these homemade gold coins have something to do with the holdups. After talking to Doc Vance, I calculated the coins started showing up shortly after the first robbery a few months ago."

"If we are able to capture him, what then?" Sandoval asked. "Just ask questions and let him go?"

"Depends on the answers we get," Charvein said. He didn't mention his earlier idea of stringing Sandoval's braided rawhide lariat across the main street to trip up the courier. Even if such a dangerous trick worked, it could very well kill or injure the horse or rider. There had to be another way. "Leave the animals saddled and hobbled. Let them graze or rest close by. We'll grab him when he starts to ride away." He paused. "Sandoval, are you still good with a rope?"

"*Sí.* In my younger days, I could hold my own with any vaquero in Sonora."

"Hope your arm and your eye are still good because I want to ride in close on both sides, and surprise him. Get your lariat on him as quick as you can before he can put up a fight. We'll likely have only one quick shot at this."

"That's if he shows up at all." Lucy stifled a yawn.

Sandoval stepped away to see about the animals. He took his coiled lariat from the saddle, shook it out, and rubbed a beeswax candle on the rawhide, testing the loop to be sure it would slip easily.

Lucy and Charvein stretched out on their blankets in a grassy area just beyond the rocks of the creek bed.

Chapter 16

"Marc! Marc!"

His own name exploded through the thick fog of sleep. Charvein jerked fully awake, noting how far the moon had traveled across the night sky.

"A horseman comes!" Sandoval hissed.

Faint hoofbeats somewhere to the east, but not close. He listened again, but the sound had vanished. "Gone." He looked toward Sandoval, who was slipping the hobbles from his mule.

"He rode down into an arroyo."

Lucy was tightening the cinch of her saddle.

By the time they were all mounted, they could see the horseman, a black silhouette some three-hundred yards distant, closing on the village. Charvein had time for only a quick look, but a chill went up his back. The black-caped rider swayed smoothly in rhythm with his horse, both of them moving as one black figure in the pale moonlight.

Charvein motioned for Sandoval and Lucy to ride down the slope of the creek bank into the inky shadows of a clump of young cottonwoods, where they reined up. The burro they left hobbled.

On came the apparition across the open desert, making no effort to hide, and Charvein got the impression the man and horse could cover miles at this easy lope without tiring. He wondered how far they had already come.

When he reached the beginning of the main street, the

mysterious rider slowed his mount to a trot and reached into saddlebags that were draped across the pommel.

From shelter of the cottonwoods, Charvein saw him rein up in front of the Fortuna house and fling something that appeared to be a tiny sack toward the door. Then he walked his horse down the main street, and repeated the action at another squat adobe.

Charvein led the way along the creek bank, their horses' hoofbeats deadened by the grass. He leaned across to Sandoval. "Head him off as he leaves town," he whispered. The gurgling of the creek and the soft rustle of a predawn breeze in the cottonwoods masked his voice.

Sandoval held his coiled lariat in one hand.

Charvein lost sight of the rider, but could see the road where it left the village and curled toward the west. He pushed his horse to a trot. Maybe the courier would turn and leave town the same way he'd come. How many deliveries did this masked rider have in San Felipe? It seemed like a long time before the three of them approached the far end of the village with no sign of him.

The dark figure appeared from behind the last building on the street. The horse was moving at a walk. Then the rider turned the animal and came directly toward them. In the moonlight, a white blaze stood out on the horse's forehead. Where was he headed? Charvein reined up and the three of them waited as the dark rider on the black horse slowly approached. *Can he see us?* No. The horse needs rest. They were upwind of the phantom rider. His horse would catch their scent in the next minute or so. Charvein held his breath and dared not speak.

The masked rider reined his mount toward a break in the line of trees bordering the creek. Of course—he was guiding the animal to water. This was even better than he'd dared hope.

Charvein glanced at his companions on either side. They'd follow his lead. He forced himself to be patient and wait until the time was right. He studied the village. No one in sight. All was still and quiet, except for the breeze that had picked up in the treetops.

The rider dismounted and walked his mount to the stream about a hundred yards beyond the edge of the village. Charvein caught himself wishing it was farther, and beyond the sight of any watchers.

While the horse thrust his muzzle into the water, the man squatted on the opposite side, apparently filling his canteen.

"Okay, now!" Charvein said quietly and kicked his horse forward. The three burst from the shelter of the dark shadows and thundered toward the horse and rider.

The man's head appeared over the back of his horse. He fumbled with something before he could grab the reins and vault into the saddle. But he'd wasted time trying to secure his canteen to the saddle horn. Charvein and Sandoval pulled up on either side, hemming him in. Charvein had his pistol in hand. "Hold it, mister!"

Sandoval grabbed the bridle; there was no need for his coiled lariat.

The rider didn't resist. He raised his hands to shoulder height.

"B'God, you can have what I got. Just don't shoot."

"Get down."

The rider complied. Afoot, he wasn't much over five and a half feet tall. While Lucy looked on, Charvein held his pistol on the rider and Sandoval slid the gun from the courier's holster, then swiftly ran his hands over the man's clothing to check for any hideout gun or knife. "Nothing but this." Sandoval shoved the man's pistol under his belt.

"All I'm carrying is in my saddlebags." He still held up his hands while he stepped back two paces.

The bags had been fashioned to loop over the saddle horn in front of the rider and Sandoval took them down with one hand while holding the man's horse with the other.

"Move out into the light," Charvein ordered, taking the saddlebags and handing them to Lucy, keeping his eyes on the man. "See what's in there." He and Lucy both dismounted and all led their horses away from the creek to where the still-bright moon was silvering the landscape.

"You stand right still and we won't hurt you," Sandoval said.

"You American bandits?" The voice from behind the hood carried some kind of a slight accent.

"We're Americans, but not bandits," Charvein said. "Take off that hood."

The man didn't hesitate, removing his hat and pulling off the black head covering. "Whew! That feels better. 'Tis hotter than Hades under that." He also unhooked the short black cape and flung it across his saddle.

"What's the point of the mask and cape?" Sandoval asked.

"B'God, I'm beginnin' to wonder m'self."

Lucy pulled out a handful of tiny rawhide sacks, each less than a third as large as the average coin purse. She opened one and a gold coin slid out, gleaming in the moonlight.

Charvein backed up and reached for it. "Keep him covered," he ordered Sandoval. He took the coin, which seemed heavy for its size, and held it closer to his eyes, tilting it toward the moonlight. The same Celtic cross on one side and an arrow on the other. It was roughly the size and weight of a U.S. $50 gold piece.

Lucy handed him two more. "Looks to be a bunch of these."

"Lower your hands, but don't make any sudden moves," Charvein said. "Who are you and why are you giving these coins to the Mexicans?"

"Robin Hood was a damned Englishman, but I fancy m'self

doing the same good work he did."

"What're you talking about?"

"If you're not going to shoot me, take the money and go."

"We're giving the orders here," Charvein said.

"Then you're keeping me a prisoner?" the man asked. "If you're not bandits, you must be the law, and you'd be haulin' me off to jail?"

"What's your name?" Charvein demanded.

"B'God, I could give you any name that comes into m'head, and you'd not know the difference. But I was baptized Michael Flaherty."

"You've got a sharp tongue for a man on the wrong end of a forty-five."

"I'll not die with a lie on m'lips," was the rejoinder. He showed no intimidation.

"There's nothing else in the saddlebags but some jerky and tortillas and a notebook and pencil," Lucy said.

"Lemme see the notebook," Charvein said. He flipped through the pages and saw a list of names with check marks beside them. Also the names and directions to four villages. Apparently, these were the benefactors of the gold distribution.

Sandoval had holstered his Colt, while the four of them stood talking near the edge of the copse of trees bordering the creek.

"You'll come with us until you begin to give straight answers to our questions," Charvein said. "What you tell us will determine if we confiscate these gold coins as evidence or whether we let you go."

Charvein heard a sudden ratcheting noise. It was no sound in nature. He stiffened, recognizing a lever action rifle being cocked. "I'd not be makin' any plans for your own near future," a raspy voice said behind him in the inky shadows.

Lucy gasped.

"Don't turn around," the deep voice said. "Just keep your

hands where we can see them. You're covered by two Winchesters."

Charvein sensed the figures moving afoot out of the shelter of the nearby trees.

"You don't think we'd let Michael, here, travel these lonely, dark roads without an escort, now do you?" another voice said. "Northern Sonora is crawling with *bandidos.*" He gave a short, harsh laugh.

Charvein's stomach fell. He silently cursed himself for not anticipating this. But it was too late now.

CHAPTER 17

The faces of the two men were shaded by their hat brims as they moved forward out of the shadows. Both appeared lean and well under six feet tall. But the gleaming carbine barrels made them seem larger.

"We've dusted off more than one bunch of bandits who thought our man was easy pickings," one of them remarked, snatching the saddlebags from Lucy's hand. "Here ya go, Michael." He tossed them to the courier. "You'd best be on your way."

Flaherty put on his hat but stuffed the hood and the short cape into the leather pockets before hooking the saddlebags over the horn. He snatched his pistol from Sandoval's belt, then swung up easily and the black horse galloped away.

"Take out your weapons and toss them over here," one of their captors ordered as the hoofbeats faded. These men had no Irish dialects. They sounded strictly like Americans.

"We're not bandits," Charvein said, as they complied. "We only wanted to ask him some questions."

"And you were going to kidnap him to do it, and maybe take some of those gold coins." One of them snorted a derisive laugh. "We heard what you said."

"Whaddya think we should do with them?" the other asked.

The second man appeared to study each of the three in turn. Lucy and Sandoval wore no hats. The moonlight revealed Lucy's dark hair and slender figure in her divided riding skirt;

Sandoval's salt and pepper collar-length hair, beardless face, and desert moccasins. "A white man, an Injun, and a woman—ain't your average highway robbers," was the reply.

They seemed undecided.

Charvein wondered if he should reveal they were working for Wells Fargo, and had no interest in robbery. If he showed them his identification badge and papers to prove the three of them were on the right side of the law, perhaps the riflemen would let them go and move on their way as rear guards for the midnight courier. But he held his tongue. That revelation might save their lives. On the other hand, it might endanger them in case these handmade gold coins *did* have a connection with the express car robberies.

The matter was decided for him when the first man said, "Empty your pockets, mister." He punctuated his command by jabbing the rifle barrel at Charvein.

Charvein's long gun was in its saddle scabbard and his pistol lay on the ground near his feet, as did Sandoval's and Lucy's. Sandoval's bowie knife was shoved under the belt of one of the men.

The contents of his pockets—bandanna, a few silver coins, comb, pencil, held no interest and one of the riflemen dropped them on the ground until Charvein handed over his billfold. The man flipped it open and moonlight shown dully on the silver badge pinned inside.

"Ah, hah! A lawman."

"Wells Fargo agent," Charvein corrected, seeing no further sense in evasion.

"The damned law! Worse than bandits."

"Shoot 'em?"

The other hesitated. "Naw. The boss made it clear there'd be no killing, except in self-defense."

"Hell, we can't just turn 'em loose."

One of the men touched the other's shoulder and motioned for him to step away a few yards to confer in private.

"Don't think we ain't watchin' you." He held the carbine steady. "Any sudden moves and you get a bullet."

The pair leaned together and held a whispered conversation.

Charvein looked aside at Sandoval and Lucy. Sandoval slowly shook his head, indicating he had no idea what would happen next. They were at the mercy of these two outriders.

Charvein had begun to doubt his abilities as a Wells Fargo detective. He should have been aware a nightrider who was known to travel with gold coins would not be making his rounds alone without protection.

Their captors broke up their discussion and returned. One of them, who appeared to be the leader, picked up the three pistols from the ground, shoved Sandoval's Colt conversion under his belt, and handed Lucy's .38 to his companion. Charvein's weapon he glanced at a second time and then held it up to the moonlight and examined it more carefully.

"Where'd you get this?" he demanded.

Charvein didn't reply.

"Hell! This is Ward Conley's Webley-Pryse .45. See—it's got his initials, 'WC,' carved in tiny letters on the bottom of the grip." He held up the pistol for his companion to see in the moonlight.

"He brought it with him when he come over the water," the other added.

The first man gestured with the British-made revolver. "We're taking you three to the boss. He'll likely have some ideas about what to do with you. I think you're going to regret ever messing with our nightrider."

The two captors collected the horses they'd tied on the opposite side of the creek in a thick stand of small trees. They gave orders for all the animals to be watered in the creek and the canteens filled before the party mounted and rode away cross-country to the southwest. Charvein's rifle rested in the captor's saddle scabbard while the man carried his own carbine across the saddle bows. Charvein, Sandoval, and Lucy rode abreast, while their captors, whose faces still had not been seen in the deep shadows of their hat brims, rode on either side of the three and slightly to the rear.

After galloping for a mile, they were ordered to walk their animals for a time. Then they rode at an easy canter for another mile before reining back to a walk. After roughly five miles at this alternating pace, they stood down to walk, stretching their legs and leading the horses to cool them down.

The moon faded and rugged mountains that had seemed distant began to draw gradually closer and clearer in the first hint of a gray dawn. The pace slowed as they carefully worked their way in and out of dry arroyos that gashed the desert landscape—remnants of flash floods that had roared out of the mountain canyons in times past.

They were traveling deeper into Mexico in a southwesterly direction, and had seen no other villages or roads since leaving San Felipe. Charvein wondered if Diego, or any of the watching Mexicans, had seen what happened to them. It was possible no one had observed them accosting the courier, or their own capture, because the events had taken place mostly in the deep shadows of the creek bank a quarter mile from the western end of the village. If anyone *had* seen the confrontation, they'd either not guessed what was happening, or had chosen not to interfere. In any case, they could hardly expect the poor residents of the town to band together and come to their rescue.

Charvein's boots dug into reddish dirt, sliding, as he tried to pull his horse to the rim of yet another deep arroyo. With one last lunge, the horse gained the top.

He glanced ahead at the gray flank of the rocky upthrust two miles ahead. They were moving into mountainous country that to Charvein was totally unfamiliar. They were not the first indications of the Sierra Madres, which were miles to the east. He took a deep breath of the rapidly heating air. It was fresh, wild country with only widely scattered Mexican settlements for many miles around.

He rubbed the horse's head between the ears, his mind jumping ahead. What awaited them? Would any of the three get out of these mountains alive? It apparently depended on the decision of this mysterious "boss." He glanced at the rugged flank of the mountain that was beginning to show its seams and scars in the strengthening light.

Looking back at the others following, he could make out the features of the two men who were driving them. One was a sunburned blond man, with a peeling nose that topped a drooping, tobacco-stained mustache.

The other had at least a five-day growth of black stubble on his face, with untrimmed dark hair thrusting out in all directions from under his hat. Squint-eyed, and with a gash for a mouth, his was a grim expression that gave no clue to his state of mind.

"Hold up here," the dark one said, pausing at the top to wipe his face with a sleeve. He reached for the canteen on his saddle and the others did the same.

Charven tipped up his canteen and took two swallows before capping it again.

"No need to save it," the grim man remarked, seeing this action. "There's more water in a little spring up yonder in the hills about three miles. In fact, we can give the horses a drink."

All of them poured water into their hats. The thirsty animals sucked up the inadequate amount. Charvein's horse nuzzled him for more.

"That's it for now, fella. Hang on a little longer."

"Who're you talkin' to?" the blond man snapped, coming up beside him, huffing and red-faced.

Charvein ignored the question.

"We'll ride 'til it gets too steep and then lead the animals the rest of the way," the dark man said, jabbing a finger toward the mountain ahead.

Sandoval mounted his mule and led out. There was not even a game trail to follow, but the animals fell into single file behind Jeremiah, the sure-footed mule who picked his way along the steepening rocky incline. The creosote bushes thinned out and the saguaro grew less frequent. It was amazing how big these desert mountains were when one got close to them. From miles away, they appeared to be only gray, jagged walls on the horizon, giving no real sense of their size.

"Just keep going. You'll see a trail when you get close," the dark man told Sandoval. "A deep gash to the left of that peak."

Their pace slowed, and the sun rose and grew hotter on their backs in the windless air.

They were within thirty yards of the giant cleft before they saw the trail, which opened up between two massive boulders. The ascent flattened out until it was very gradual, and shortly they were riding into a narrow canyon. A graveled creek bed carried a slight trickle of water as they wound into the heart of the mountain. The trail curved slightly and giant rock walls rose up on either side, shutting off the sunlight. The steady clopping of shod hooves on solid rock echoed off the granite walls. Charvein relished the cool air, but reflected this would be a bad place to be caught in a flash flood. He noticed hoofprints in the damp sand, and some fresh manure. There were also piles of disintegrating dung that looked to be weeks old. This narrow canyon was obviously the main way in and out of wherever they were headed.

He didn't have long to wonder. Another quarter mile around a sweeping curve brought them abruptly back into full daylight. A valley opened before them. They had apparently passed through the first barrier of mountains into this several-acre open space ringed on three sides by the rocky hillsides. The grassy valley sloped gently downward to the desert floor beyond. Then, across a half-mile of desert were the jagged teeth of more low mountains. Several horses grazed on a wide grassy strip near the row of stunted cottonwoods that marked the flow of the unseen water. Charvein assumed the small creek was actually a year-round mountain spring.

In the middle of this cove stood a one-story adobe dwelling with a flat roof supported by protruding cottonwood beams. The walls, plastered with clay, were weathered and cracked. As their tired animals approached at a walk, Charvein noted the angles of several additional rooms that appeared to have been added haphazardly over time. A tumbledown corral of stacked rocks stood apart on the upper side. Downslope from the main building was another roofless rock structure that was emitting a thin column of wood smoke. A wagon was parked next to its wall.

Charvein wondered why the cooking fire wasn't in the main building, then realized it was likely too hot to cook indoors.

Three men came out of the open doorway and squinted at them in the morning sunlight. None of them was wearing a hat. And, in spite of their rugged surrounding in this remote location, all of them were clean-shaven and neatly groomed. Their jeans and cotton shirts appeared to be clean.

Charvein's party and their two captors reined up and dismounted on the hard-packed clay a few yards in the front of the building. There was no hitching rack, but the ground-reined animals made no move to wander off.

The dark man motioned with a pistol for Charvein, Lucy,

and Sandoval to move up next to the wall of the building.

"Boss here?" the blond one asked.

"Inside." The man jerked a thumb over his shoulder while eyeing Lucy.

The dark man entered and was gone for a couple of minutes. "Bring them in," he said when he returned.

The blond drew his revolver and motioned for the three to move ahead of him. They passed through a small room that contained only two chairs and a bedroll lying next to a wall. The shutters of the glassless windows stood open to the early breeze. It seemed pleasantly cool inside the insulating adobe.

Sandoval and Lucy followed Charvein into the smaller room. A man behind a plain wooden table got up from his breakfast and turned to face them.

Charvein heard Lucy gasp.

CHAPTER 18

The man who stood silently regarding them was probably the handsomest man Charvein had ever seen. He glanced sideways at Lucy whose eyes were riveted on this Adonis.

The "boss" had black hair and eyebrows, startling blue eyes, and a fair complexion only slightly darkened by exposure to the sun. Perhaps a shade under six feet tall, he was probably the shy side of forty, lean and athletic looking. Only a hint of dark beard showed on his clean-shaven flat cheeks. He had a straight nose and firm chin, and could have graced an advertising poster or a stage anywhere in the states or Mexico.

Charvein half-expected him to launch into a Shakespearian soliloquy, but he only asked a mundane question of Lucy, "How long has it been since you ate?"

"Uh . . . It's a . . ." she stammered at the unexpected question from this vision.

"Some tortillas and beans at sunset last night," Sandoval answered.

The man turned to the dark captor. "Logan, bring these people something to eat and a pot of coffee. And set another chair in here."

"Yessir."

Only then did Charvein notice they had interrupted the man's breakfast of steak, tortillas, and beans. A revolver lay on the table near his plate. At a quick glance, it looked to be Charvein's Webley-Pryse. In a minute they were all seated, the man behind the table and the three of them in homemade chairs facing him. He sat regarding them in silence for several seconds and Charvein had a chance to glance at the man's attire. Brown, whipcord pants were topped by a pale green shirt, open at the collar and showing a silver chain around his neck. He sat back and crossed an ankle over his knee, revealing some kind of smooth leather moccasins that appeared to be custom-made.

"Our horses and mule need water," Charvein said to break the tense silence.

"My men will see to that and also to their feed," the man replied, amiably. "We don't neglect our livestock here."

Nothing further was said for five minutes while they waited for their food. Lucy was fidgeting, but Sandoval sat, apparently at ease. Charvein saw his alert eyes darting around the room, taking in details of their surroundings. Charvein knew his half-breed friend had faced down many perilous situations, and knew how to relax when he could. Charvein would have been nervous, but was too tired from their all-night ride to think about much of anything except how good it felt to be seated in a chair. Perhaps it was this man's civil demeanor. Charvein leaned forward to stretch his back muscles. He took a deep breath of the fresh desert breeze blowing in the open window.

Their captors returned shortly with three tin plates of smoking steak, beans, and tortillas and a pot of coffee and three cups. "These are full." The blond man set three canteens on the floor beside their chairs before he and his companion left the room.

They held the plates in their laps and ate, while the handsome man finished his own interrupted breakfast in silence.

Charvein hadn't realized how hungry he was. Since he'd seen no sign of any cattle as they rode in, he wondered if the steaks could be from a horse or mule. But it tasted as good as any beef he'd ever had. He put the thought out of his mind, speculating instead about what kind of strange place this might be. Obviously, these men were engaged in some illegal activity, or they wouldn't be out in this remote, hidden location. In his brief look around as they were herded into this mountain cove, he had not spotted Michael Flaherty. If the mysterious masked rider had returned here, he was very likely off sleeping someplace after his long night ride.

At length, everyone finished eating, and the three placed their plates and forks on the floor. Their host indicated the black coffeepot on the corner of the table. "Feel free to help yourselves," he said, standing up. He faced them. "I guess it's about time I introduce myself. I'm James Gordon Flynn—a name that means nothing to you, I'm sure. I am just another poor Irish immigrant—one of more than a million who fled the Great Hunger in the 40s. Actually, I had no choice in the matter. It was my widowed mother—God rest her—who took ship from Cork, paying for our passage with borrowed money and brought me along—a babe in arms."

"You have no Irish dialect," Lucy said.

"Only a slight one from my mum. I learned to speak in America." He folded his arms across his chest. "But enough of that. Logan tells me he and Wilson caught you threatening Michael Flaherty last night near San Felipe." He looked at Charvein. "He also tells me you showed him a badge and identified yourself as a Wells Fargo agent. Correct?"

Charvein nodded. This was beginning to feel demeaning—as if he were being interrogated by a schoolmaster for making trouble in the classroom. *Why doesn't this man get to the point? One of those Irish blatherskites who enjoys hearing himself talk.*

"Logan also showed me this Webley-Pryse revolver you were armed with. I don't know where you got it, but that's a wellmade British revolver. I don't blame you for preferring it to whatever you were using before."

"You know where it came from," Charvein retorted. "I wounded one of your train robbers who dropped it when he was escaping."

Flynn shrugged. "By the saints, I've no idea what you're talking about. Some fantasy of yours, I suspect." He walked back behind the table. "As much as I hate to do it, I'll have to get down to business. First of all, I'll ask if anyone of you has anything to say—a story to tell me, perhaps. An excuse for why you accosted my rider?"

Charvein glanced at Sandoval. Who should talk first? How much should they reveal? It was apparent Flynn knew most of it. Sandoval nodded as if to say, "Go ahead."

"First of all, your arrogance is showing," Charvein said. "I think it's important to know who you're talking to. You didn't even ask our names." He introduced the three of them, and Flynn nodded to each, taking no obvious offense at the words.

"I'm a messenger for Wells Fargo in charge of the express car on the Southern Pacific." He wanted to get this said as quickly as possible. "Sandoval works for me. Lucy is an old friend of ours. She overheard some talk in Yuma and tried to warn us— too late as it turned out—of a possible ambush near Gila Bend. I can only speculate as to the reason we were shot at."

Flynn frowned, as if puzzled. "Let me say I had no knowledge of that, and regret that it happened."

"You must have very loyal men who will protect you at any cost," Lucy said, her face flushing.

"Oh, so *that's* the connection. Was my name mentioned by anyone in all of this speculation?" Flynn asked mildly.

"No," Lucy said. "But from the conversation I heard, there was some kind of plot to stop these two men from riding into Mexico in search of the bandits who've been robbing the trains."

"You think my man, Michael Flaherty, had something to do with it?"

"The coins he's been distributing to poor Mexican families are homemade," Charvein said. "I think they're minted of stolen gold from the train robberies." Being blunt might stop this charade and get at the truth. It might also get them killed.

"Hmmm . . . interesting theory. But, I suppose when one has no proof, one must make wild conjectures in an attempt to connect two unrelated incidents." His manner was still calm. "First of all, Logan and Wilson, the men who detained and guided you here, made a mistake in judgment. They should have just sent you on your way—as I will do."

Charvein fastened on this last statement with great relief.

"What, exactly, do you do here?" Sandoval asked.

"I run a private company with a dozen or so men. What we do is none of your affair. We should be commended for sharing our profits by distributing gold coins to the poor. Would that others had the means and will to do the same."

"What sort of legitimate company makes that kind of profit?" Charvein asked.

"I'm not obliged to tell you, but I will—just to quell your suspicions. I have had the great good fortune to strike a rich vein of gold. It is a legal claim. But since it's located here in Sonora, I felt morally bound to share some of it with the poorest of the peasants."

"What's with the all the mask, the black cape, and night-riding?" Sandoval asked.

He smiled, showing a row of white teeth. "Just a whim of mine. A flair for the dramatic, if you will. I fear some of these peasants are superstitious to the point that when they see a man in a black cape riding in the moonlight, they begin to suspect the devil. But, does the devil do good works? I think most of these poor people are grateful for the largesse. They don't understand where it comes from—possibly manna from heaven—but they accept it with a prayer of thanks and don't look a gift horse in the mouth—as you three are doing."

This man was cultured and spoke with the vocabulary of a college graduate. Charvein wondered about his background.

"Juan Fortuna in San Felipe was shot and nearly killed by bandits who were trying to take his gold." Sandoval rose and refilled his tin coffee cup. "His wife thinks the gold is bad luck and won't speak about it."

Flynn shrugged. "Luck has nothing to do with it. This country is full of road agents. Word of our little distribution has gotten around, and Mexican bandits are quick to pick up on such things. It's an unfortunate fact of life. I can't control everything."

The man was charming and would have made an excellent salesman, Charvein reflected. He was also very convincing, and Charvein might have been tempted to believe him—except for one detail: the rough-looking man named Logan last night had taken one look at the Webley-Pryse revolver and blurted out that it belonged to a man named Ward Conley, and had identified it by the initials in the butt.

"Sorry your search for those . . . train bandits . . . has led you far off-track into a box canyon here," Flynn said. "But I'm not sorry we're not the ones you're seeking. Just the opposite, in fact. We distribute gold—we don't take it." He smiled. "But now I must attend to a few things. My men will provide you with food and water and whatever you need to see you back to the border, or to San Felipe or wherever you might be going. If you want to rest yourselves and your animals before you start, there is decent grass and water just west of here a few miles. That stream then will disappear underground, so get what water you need at that point."

This was certainly not the reception Charvein had been braced for. It was like taking a punch at an opponent—and missing, throwing himself badly off-balance. But he quickly recovered. They'd have to regroup. "Thanks for your hospitality, Mister Flynn," he said, with studied formality, not offering his hand. "We'll have our guns back before we leave."

"Certainly. All except this Webley. Call it payment for provisions. I think I might want to use it myself."

They smiled at each other, Charvein silently acknowledging that he'd just been done out of the main physical link between the robberies and Flynn. Knowing he could not press the issue at the moment, he followed Sandoval and Lucy out the door.

"While we were talking, your animals have been rubbed down and fed," Flynn said when they were outside in the hot midmorning sun. "I'll have my men saddle them for you and escort you down the valley to the camping site I spoke of."

Lucy was frowning and looking at Charvein as if she expected him to say something. But he caught her eye and shook his head.

As they gathered up their horses and weapons, Charvein tried to see as much of this operation as he could. Without checking, he knew their Winchesters and sidearms had been unloaded.

The stocky, dark-haired Logan mounted and led them down the sloping valley. As they passed the roofless rock structure with the fire, he saw three sweaty men moving around some kind of forge. But he caught only a brief glance as they passed and couldn't make out what they were doing. It looked almost like a blacksmith operation. Were they just fashioning horseshoes or wheel rims for wagons? An operation this remote from any towns would need a forge to make or repair their own hardware. If Flynn was telling at least a partial truth, that was also a smelting operation for their mined ore, and a hand-stamping mint for the gold coins they distributed.

Three miles later, Logan reined up and pointed at a bend in the small stream where an acre of grass grew on the flat land.

Then he silently wheeled his horse and started back. The small valley with its adobe buildings had been hidden from sight around a bulge of the mountain for at least two miles.

CHAPTER 19

Several minutes after the masked rider disappeared from San Felipe, Diego slid out of his hiding place in the cottonwoods near the creek, and gazed after five riders galloping away to the southwest. Before the silhouettes receded in the moonlight, he recognized the shapes of the three visitors—the slight woman with the long hair, the small man named Sandoval, and the gringo who seemed to be their leader. But who were the other two? He had a bad feeling in his stomach they were a couple of *bandidos.*

He trotted along the rocky creek bank, his sandals slapping on the flat stone shelf, toward the spot where he had eaten with the three visitors. They were gone. But the burro Sandoval had called Lupida was still there, hobbled and grazing. Were the three coming back to get this animal? They were galloping away as if they had a purpose—a destination in mind. He paused, trying to puzzle out the situation. If they had been captured by *bandidos,* it had been very quiet—no shouting, no shots fired. But why would robbers even want them? Hostages? If the two extra riders were dreaded brigands, why not rob the masked rider? He was the one who had the gold. It didn't make any sense.

He went up to the burro, speaking very softly. She raised her head and twitched her ears. He reached out his hand and rubbed her pale nose. At first she pulled away from him, but the hobbles allowed only an awkward hop.

"Ah . . . Lupida . . . good girl." Then she stood and allowed herself to be petted. After a minute or two she nuzzled him as if looking for a carrot, but then dropped her head and continued grazing.

What should he do? Tell his boss about Lupida? The blacksmith would only sell her and keep the money if the three did not return within a few days.

No. He would keep her as his own transportation. She was gentle and would also be a friend. He had few enough of those.

Looking around the site, he found a wooden packsaddle that had also been left behind. Sandoval was a Mexican, like himself, and Diego felt a kinship with him that he did not feel for the other two gringos. Sandoval would not have left such an animal behind if he did not intend to return soon. That gave Diego a very uneasy feeling that the three he'd shared food and beer with, and confided the tale of the nightrider, had not ridden away of their own accord with two mysterious men who had shown up out of nowhere. Even though he had not seen their faces, he felt these two mysterious figures were not men from San Felipe. When daylight came, he would find out for sure. Were all five of them chasing the masked courier? His instinct told him they were not. But then he had a thought that the two additional riders might have been men they had arranged to meet when the nightrider showed up. They were extra help to capture this distributor of gold coins.

A possibility, but he dismissed the thought as unlikely. If they didn't return for the burro in a day or two, he'd know they'd been taken by force. He felt it in his bones. He had lived all his life in this village and knew the ways of Mexican *bandidos*.

He felt the predawn breeze and knew he had to quickly make up his mind. He would take Lupida to his secret hiding place in a nearby mountain. There was a small spring that fed down into the nearby creek. And there was enough grass and shrubbery for her to eat until he knew if Sandoval would return for her. He had not even taken the younger Fortuna boy into his confidence about this secret place. It was over a mile distant toward the border. It was where he retreated when he had to be alone, did not want to be found—a safe haven where he could think, and escape the brutality of his boss and unofficial foster father, Juan Gomez.

He took off her hobbles and led her across the shallow creek. Once they were clear of the row of trees and brush, he began to jog, leading her by her halter. She followed him willingly across the desert still lighted by a moon that was ducking in and out of high clouds.

There was no great hurry. He had at least three hours before he was due at work.

Once in his hidden alcove, he replaced her hobbles so she wouldn't try to follow him back. She would be safe there until he could check on her the following evening.

By the time he reached the village again, he was nearly falling asleep on his feet. He'd been up all night, and now had to work all day as an apprentice for a very hard boss on a very hot job. He splashed in the cool water of the creek to refresh himself and then went to lie down and sleep for an hour or so in the grass before the sun woke him to another day of drudgery.

CHAPTER 20

Charvein dragged the saddle and blanket from his horse and dumped them on the ground in the shade of a large cotton-wood.

The other two had already begun to settle in. Sandoval took his lariat and picketed all three animals between two trees where they could reach the water and still had adequate browse.

Charvein had a long drink from the creek and then soused his head in the cool water. His eyes were gritty from the sun and lack of sleep, his limbs heavy with fatigue. Wiping his face on his shirtsleeve, he said, "Before I even think about what we should do next, I'm going to get some sleep and clear my head. And our mounts need rest as much as we do."

"Good idea." Lucy brushed her hair out of her eyes as a hot noon breeze gusted into their tiny oasis from the sun-blasted desert.

"No need to keep watch." Sandoval sat down on his blanket and took off his gunbelt. "But just in case . . ." he continued, as he began loading his pistol. "It's good to be prepared." His carbine lay beside him.

Lucy followed his example, shoving cartridges into her .38. Charvein had no pistol, but loaded his Winchester. At least Flynn had left their extra ammunition.

None of them seemed inclined to talk. Coping with problems was never easy, and Charvein found it an effort to even think when he was mentally and physically fatigued. He stretched out on his ground cover in the cool shade and let the burble of water over the rocks and the soft rushing of windblown cottonwood leaves lull him into a deep sleep.

When he awoke, the sun was nearly resting on the top of a gray rocky wall of low mountains. He stretched and yawned, coming awake gradually. He had needed that, and felt rested. Glancing at the animals, he noted Sandoval had moved the slack picket line to a fresh grassy area. The mule was grazing and the two horses lying down.

His two companions still slept. Good. Let them. Charvein got up and checked his saddlebags. Flynn was as good as his word. The bags contained a small sack of coffee beans and some hard bread. Melting grease was soaking a burlap wrap that contained a side of bacon. Digging out the food and coffeepot, he considered how much trouble Flynn had gone to in his attempts to throw them off the trail. Charvein even found a plain gold disc in the bottom of the bag. The Irishman was trying to kill them with kindness—or bribe them with it so they wouldn't come back.

He pondered this while he gathered some dry brush from along the creek for a small cooking fire. The late afternoon breeze had died, and it took only one match to kindle the tinder.

An hour later, Charvein leaned back on his saddle, full of the enemy's food and coffee, and feeling much revived for it. "What's our next move?"

"I think we should go back there," Lucy said.

"And do what?"

"I don't know. I'm just frustrated that he treated me . . . us . . . like children—patted us on the heads and sent us off to play. As a woman, I've had to put up with that kind of condescending attitude most of my growing-up years."

Charvein looked at Sandoval. "What about you?"

"We'd be foolish to return there now and probably get ourselves shot." Sandoval leaned on one elbow on his blanket. "If there was such thing as law in this remote part of Sonora, Flynn could just say he warned us not to come back, and then shot us as trespassers and potential thieves when we did."

"Well, he has the Webley revolver—the only piece of physical evidence I had connecting a train robber to one of his men. And if there is a man named Ward Conley walking around there, we certainly didn't know which one he was. We have only a couple of remarks made by that Logan character and his friend Wilson," Charvein said.

They were silent with their own thoughts for a minute.

"We don't know for sure how many men they have there," Sandoval said. "We're certainly outnumbered and outgunned. If they're smelting stolen gold and minting coins for profit and charity, how do we prove it or stop them?" He wondered aloud.

"If it helps at all, I just remembered something else about that conversation I overheard between the telegrapher and his friend," Lucy said. "A couple of times they called the boss 'Face.' "

"Well, you can certainly see why Flynn might have that nickname," Charvein said. "I notice you thought he was a very handsome man as well," he added, with a slight smile.

Lucy's color deepened under her windburn. "Handsome is as handsome does," she quoted.

"Well, so far he's done nothing to belie that," Charvein said. "In fact, just the opposite. He's been every inch the generous gentleman."

"We all know it was just an act." Lucy was clearly frustrated.

"*Sí*. But as long as we have no evidence of wrongdoing, it's good cover," Sandoval said.

"If we could only catch one of the robbers in the act . . . and make him talk," Charvein muttered. "Armed robbery is a dangerous game. Flynn's men must be well paid if they'll continue to risk their lives for him. Sooner or later one of them is bound to be caught or killed."

"Hasn't happened so far," Sandoval observed. "That's why we're here. Wells Fargo won't wait any longer."

"But our mission *has* been a success," Charvein insisted, trying to draw something positive out of the past few days. "We now know where the gold is brought for smelting. And we've established the connection between this night-riding 'Robin Hood' and that bunch back there."

"Since all of us are in Sonora on our own, maybe you should ask Wells Fargo or the U.S. Government to request the help of the Mexican *Federales*," Lucy suggested. "With the information we have, they'd probably cooperate."

Charvein shook his head. "Coughlin was adamant about not getting outside help. His job with Wells Fargo is on the line and he has only a few more months until he can retire. He wants to handle this internally. He especially didn't want the Pinkertons involved. It's something to do with his pride when it comes to them." He took a stick and poked up the dying fire. "I'm guessing Flynn is too smart for anything like that. If some official law enforcement or detective agency came snooping around, his scouts would alert him days in advance and he'd just fold his tent and disappear."

Sandoval blew through the stem of his pipe, then began thumbing rough-cut tobacco into the bowl. "What I do not understand," he said as he applied a blazing stick and puffed out an aromatic billow, "is why they are doing this."

"What do you mean?"

"What's their motive?"

"Gain."

"I'm thinking it is something more than that. If it is strictly for profit, is Flynn giving away part of it to the poor just to soothe a guilty conscience?"

"It's happened before," Charvein said. "Ask Lucy. She knows the history of lords and knights centuries ago who were weighed down by all their ill-gotten booty, then tried to buy their way out of hell or purgatory by building churches and endowing monasteries."

"Very common." She nodded. "Human nature. They want it now and they want it later, too."

"I still feel we don't know the whole story," Sandoval said. "I think there is something bigger here."

After several seconds, Charvein said, "As I see it, we have two choices. We must either capture one of the robbers with the loot, or we have to slip back into that valley and try to find some of the gold jewelry before it's melted down."

"The *bandidos* always work in pairs." Sandoval sat cross-legged on his blanket. "And we have no idea when they might strike next. It could be tomorrow, or it could be a month from now. So, in order to lay a trap for one or both, we would have to camp somewhere near—someplace out of sight where we can use field glasses to watch that narrow trail we came in on."

"Or, they could just as easily come in from this side of the mountain," Lucy pointed out.

"We don't have the time or the supplies to camp for some indefinite period," Charvein said. "And there's always the chance they'd spot us."

"Then I will go back into that den of thieves," Sandoval said.

"Why you?" Charvein asked.

"I am smaller, darker, quicker, and can disappear like an Indian into the landscape," he replied. "Remember, I took care of Breem Canto when that bounty hunter was stalking me. Besides," he added, "if I should not return, no one would miss me."

155

"I would," Charvein said.

"Me, too," Lucy added.

"*Gracias, amigos,* but I have been mostly alone in the world since my wife died. I have learned to take care of myself. You two need each other, and Wells Fargo needs you, too."

"I think I should go," Charvein said.

"No. It's decided," Sandoval said. "I need you here to rescue me if things go wrong. But I will be in and out before tomorrow sunrise."

"You want to try it tonight?"

"Yes. The quicker the better. I either find something or I don't. If there is no gold jewelry there, then we have lost nothing. It is worth a try."

"A long shot. It might all be melted by now. How long ago was that last robbery?"

Sandoval shrugged. "For all we know there might have been another one since we got a send-off from Gila Bend."

"You think it's just going to be lying around where you can pick it up?"

"I am guessing they feel safe in that hideout. They will not be locking things up in a big safe—even if they have one out here—like some assay office in town . . ."

"Unless to protect it from the natural greed of their own men," Lucy interrupted.

"*Si.* I had not considered that. But, I will find out soon enough. Flynn will not be expecting us to return so soon. That is not a fortress. I will be able to get past any sentries."

"We should go together to defend each other," Charvein said.

"No. One man has a better chance. And I am that man."

His tone spoke finality.

"That broken arm isn't healed yet." Charvein jabbed a finger at the dirty brace that still protected Sandoval's forearm.

The small man unstrapped it and carefully slid it off. He

flexed his fingers. "It feels good."

"Maybe so, but one good whack on that thing, even with the brace on, would put you out of action."

"It's not my gun hand," he countered. "And I don't aim to get close enough to do any arm wrestling."

"All right," Charvein conceded. Sandoval was slippery, agile, quick, and fearless. He was the logical one. "But what we need to do right now is saddle up and ride away from here. I'm sure Face has one or two men posted as lookouts to make sure we leave the area."

"Then I will return under cover of darkness." Sandoval rose from his blanket and knocked the dottle out of his pipe against the heel of his hand. *"Vamanos."*

CHAPTER 21

A mile north of Flynn's headquarters, along the same low mountain, was a place Charvein dubbed "Point of rocks" as soon as he saw it. A peculiar rock formation jutted out fifty feet from the flank of the mountain like a flying buttress from the wall of a cathedral. It was here they dropped Sandoval just after dark.

"We'll meet you here. If you're not back by daylight, Lucy and I'll hunker down out of sight until sundown," Charvein said. "If you have trouble and need help, fire three quick shots and we'll come fast."

Sandoval nodded, wondering if he would ever see his friends again.

"Here, take my lighter .38 Smith & Wesson," Lucy said. "It's a double action, easy to use."

Sandoval shook his head. "I'm used to my long-barreled Colt. It's a little heavier, but if I have to get at it quick, I won't have to think about it. Besides, your .38 is a five-shot and it's nickel-plated and that'd reflect the light."

Without another word, Sandoval cat-footed away into the darkness.

Twenty minutes later, he approached the open end of the cove where they had ridden out that morning. He paused when he saw firelight reflecting off the rocks nearby. An approach from this direction would be impossible. He would have to somehow get above, where he could get an overhead view of the operation and decide how to get inside without being seen. He looked up at the dark mountainside. It would be tough, but he thought he could do it.

The steep climb was so arduous, he had to crawl on hands and knees, gripping small mesquite bushes with his good right arm to pull himself up. He paused several times to rest, imagining his heavy breathing could be heard by the men in the valley below. His heart thumped in his ears in the silence.

When he was high enough, he bore to his right, feeling with moccasined feet before putting his weight down, fearful of dislodging any loose stones. He finally reached a vantage point where he could observe the open cove below him.

Hunkering down, he focused the field glasses on every aspect of the layout. A stone corral ten yards from the smelter might provide some cover to approach. But it was the light from the fires and the fact that the men were apparently working during the cool hours of the night that made him hesitate. The smelter was his goal. If the men were actively melting down gold to mint coins, they had to have some of the gold jewelry close at hand. And that's what he needed as evidence—at least one piece of jewelry that could be identified as being part of a Grindell Wells Fargo shipment.

Approaching from behind the corral would be risky. And there was a good chance the several horses confined there would sense his presence and begin to snort and mill about.

But the main problem was too much light. There was a fire inside the roofless walls of the smelter. And another blaze between the tumbledown walls and the adobe house lit up the area like daylight.

When did these men sleep? Maybe they worked in shifts. How many of them were there? He could pick out at least five who were up and active well after midnight. He didn't see Flynn. The boss was probably asleep in the adobe house, along with a few others. Too many guns belonging to men who knew how to use them. The odds were not good. Maybe he should forget this and go back to tell Charvein he couldn't find a way in that posed even the slimmest chance of snatching some of the jewelry and getting safely away. They'd have to find another way.

He pondered the situation for a few minutes. He dismissed the idea of approaching the cove from the eastern side. The narrow canyon trail was hemmed in by rock walls. If the alarm were raised, a man on foot wouldn't have a chance. Besides, he felt sure they'd have a lookout posted to watch that direction.

Perhaps if he created a distraction . . . After a few minutes of watching and thinking, he hit on an idea.

Moving slowly and carefully, he retraced his steps. Climbing and sliding down the steep incline was even more difficult to do quietly than coming up. But he reached the bottom quicker. Pausing to catch his breath, he cat-footed in a wide circle in the darkness to come up behind the stone and adobe horse corral not far from the shelter of trees near the stream. He checked his Colt and then felt in his pocket for a handful of loose cartridges. He uncased the field glasses and studied the layout. The bare stone walls formed a partial rectangle around the gold-melting operation. Firelight flickered off the rock walls and he could just make out shadows of men moving around inside. The larger fire in the open was a few yards beyond, blazing brightly. The strap for the binoculars was looped around his neck. He cased them and tucked them inside his shirt.

Moving with the infinite patience of his Indian ancestors, he crept toward the corral, pausing every few seconds to freeze in position for several minutes. There was virtually no wind, so he could only hope the horses did not catch his scent. He reached the gap in the adobe corral where a gate would have been. Only three peeled poles resting on hooks enclosed the opening. He eased one end off the hook and let it down soundlessly onto the ground. Then he did the same for each of the other two, hoping they didn't all fall with a clatter.

A horse whickered and tossed his head, moving within four feet of him. Another snorted. He smelled them and heard them moving restlessly. They sensed his presence. He had to hurry. The risky part would be crossing the open space, unseen. He watched until the men's shadows moved away from the edge of the crumbling rock wall. He heard indistinct voices, a metallic clanging, then a hissing sound.

Crouching low, he scuttled across the ten yards of open ground to the base of the wall, and paused, holding his breath. Then, creeping along to the edge, he peeked around at the shooting flames another thirty feet away that lit the entire open space. He waited until his breathing and heart rate steadied, then scooped a handful of .45 cartridges from his pocket. Picking the right moment, he dashed across to the fire and tossed the shells into the blaze, and ran back toward the corral.

"Hey!"

He ignored the shout behind him as he kicked the corral poles and they fell.

"An Injun!"

A shot blasted and the bullet whined off into the darkness.

"He's after the horses!"

Yells and clatter as the men dropped their tools and dashed toward the corral, drawing their guns.

"Get him! Stop those horses!"

Three of the panicked horses found their way through the opening.

Sandoval dashed around the far side of the corral and back toward the smelter. He rushed inside, squinting in the sudden firelight. A quick look around showed him nothing.

Then the cartridges in the fire began to explode like popcorn, bullets whizzing in every direction.

"Goddam! An attack!"

The roar of gunfire obscured the wild shouting.

"Stop the horses!"

"That way! Shots from that way!" Two men dashed back toward the fire, shooting. Sandoval threw himself under a wooden table as they rushed past. Then he jumped up and forced himself to pause and look carefully. There—a wooden box on the ground, piled with gold jewelry. He grabbed a filigree necklace and thrust it into his pocket, then sprang outside, yanking his Colt.

"Apaches!" somebody screamed.

Sandoval whirled and came face to face with a wide-eyed man. With a backhanded sweep of his arm, Sandoval caught the man's ear with the long barrel of his pistol. The man went down and Sandoval dashed toward the corral. He rammed a shoulder into a man's back and sent him tumbling into the running horses. Sandoval grabbed a horse's mane and flung himself up onto his back, kicking the animal's ribs with moccasined heels. The startled animal leapt over the fallen man and bolted toward the darkness of the desert.

Just then, something slammed into his right side like an iron fist. He gasped and leaned forward, knowing he was hit. He gripped the mane and clamped his knees against the heaving flanks. Distance! Distance! He tried to let himself flow up and down with the movement of the galloping horse. In less than a minute, the numbing blow to his side came alive in burning, searing pain and he reached his left hand across to feel it. His shirt was wet with blood. He gripped the mane with both hands and ducked his head, holding on.

Slowly he began to feel light-headed and dizzy. How long he rode, or in which direction, he didn't know, but the galloping horse finally slowed to a walk. By this time, his head was reeling. It had to be shock and loss of blood, he realized. He felt himself growing weaker and took a deep breath. The pain was now a deep, dull ache. That was the last thing he remembered before he began to lose control. His arms and legs went limp and he felt himself falling into a black hole.

CHAPTER 22

It was the backhanded blow across the mouth that finally decided him.

Diego scrabbled back on the dirt floor to escape another heavy clout from the infuriated Gomez, who stood over him, heavy brows beetling into one black line.

"Look! Look, you clumsy idiot! See what you've done?" He held up the smoldering pair of new leather gloves.

"It slipped! I didn't . . . mean to." Diego's voice trembled in spite of himself. The glowing horseshoe lay on the dirt floor, an accusing red eye, where it had fallen after searing large holes in the new gloves. The huge blacksmith snatched up the iron shoe with a pair of tongs and thrust it back into the coals.

Diego tasted blood and put a hand to his mouth. He could wiggle a tooth with his finger.

"You know how many pesos these cost?" Gomez boomed, venting his rage by clanging the tongs down on the forge. *"Madre de Dios!"*

Diego struggled to his feet and spat blood. *This must be what hell is like,* he thought. Smothering hot every day, even in winter, a hairy, sweaty, bald master yelling at him, striking him if he made the slightest mistake. What few clothes he owned were always peppered with small holes from flying sparks.

He stood, knees trembling, from the shock of the beast's sudden outburst.

Gomez had his back to him. "G'wan! Get out of my sight.

Go eat your damned lunch, or something."

Grateful for the reprieve, Diego untied his apron and dropped it, backing out from under the overhang into the baking village street. In spite of the glaring noonday sun, a dry wind washed over his sweaty body, providing cooling relief compared to where he'd spent the last five hours. It was heaven.

Followed by the eyes of curious bystanders, Diego moved on unsteady legs toward the cantina where he always went to buy spicy chili frijoles wrapped in a tortilla for lunch. Even when he had nothing left in his pocket until a slim payday, the bartender, a kindly old man, gave him credit. Today he was able to pay, and took his lunch out onto the shaded porch where he sat on a vacant bench to eat. His mind was in a whirl, and he barely heard the greetings of two men who passed down the sidewalk. The loosened tooth was sore when he chewed on it.

When he finished eating, he walked down to the other end of the street and out into the desert for a ways to a trash pile that was the village dump. No overpowering odor here. The garbage, and what little refuse the villagers disposed of, rarely decomposed. It either didn't change or withered up and dried out in the desert sun. He carefully poked around with a stick among the tin cans until he found what he was after—a frayed piece of rope about ten feet long. He coiled it up and jogged away toward the creek.

At this time of day, no one was there to draw water in buckets for baths or cooking. And the social gathering of women washing clothes did not take place until late afternoon when cooling shadows slid across the pale, flat rocks.

Without hesitation, he waded into the stream. At its deepest point here, the water was three feet and moving about three kilometers per hour. When he reached the other side, he sat down in a shallow area, allowing the water to flow past his chest, washing his body, his ragged pants and shirt, and soothing his feet in their leather sandals.

He'd been thinking of leaving for some time, but the backhanded blow from Gomez had told him the time was now. He had no possessions, nothing to take, and nowhere to go. He had no living relatives, and the only job open to him was apprentice to a brutal blacksmith. He was healthy and growing, and couldn't picture himself begging from those who had only slightly more than he did. So nothing could be lost by running away. Besides what he wore, his only personal possession was a sturdy clasp knife one of the men of the village had given him when Diego admired the way the old man could whittle. Perhaps this was all he needed. Perhaps he could find work in another village within walking distance—someplace away from here where he could be happy.

While sitting in the flowing stream, he put his mouth to the surface and drank and drank, as much as he could hold. A few minutes later, he repeated it until he was completely full, relaxed, and cool. Then he climbed up the bank, and began walking toward his secret hiding place where Lupida awaited him. He would not have to walk to the next village. He was now the proud owner of a beautiful, gentle burro who would carry him.

But, even before he had walked the mile to the hidden place where she was hobbled, he knew he could not ride off on another man's animal. He had to at least make an effort to find Sandoval, the proper owner.

Diego knew in his heart the three had not ridden off voluntarily, or they would not have left Lupida behind.

The burro flapped her ears and nuzzled him for a treat as he took off her hobbles. She had been grazing and resting since early this morning, and there had been plenty of shade. He petted and talked to her as if she were an old friend. Indeed, now that he was lighting out, she was his *only* friend.

He had not even a burlap sack for a saddle and the wooden packsaddle still lay by the creek. But it was no good for riding anyway. He was young and strong and would have to make do. It would be less weight for the little animal to carry. Besides, he was thinner and lighter than Sandoval, too, so Lupida should have no trouble.

He doubled the frayed piece of heavy cord and tied it to the burro's halter, then led her down from the hidden pocket in the mountain. They made a wide circle of at least a mile around San Felipe. Then he crossed back over the creek out of sight of the village before he mounted and guided her in a southwesterly direction. There were no roads, but he knew the general directions from having grown up in the area and could guide by the sun and the mountains.

An hour later, he found what he sought—the unmistakable hoofprints of five horses—or, in this case, four horses and a mule. It was good they were not following some hard-packed road or he could never have tracked them.

He didn't know where the party of five was going, or how far ahead they were, but he'd travel as long as possible in daylight, then camp in the mountains. With luck and diligence, maybe he could locate that small spring his father had shown him long ago—if it was still trickling. After that, if he hadn't caught up, he must decide how far to continue following them. From scanty information he'd picked up in the village, only a vast desert wilderness spread out before him. There was rumored to be another village about sixty or seventy kilometers in this direction, but he'd never been there. And much farther beyond that lay Puerto Peñasco, the dirt-street village on the great waters of the Sea of Cortez. But one thing was certain—he would never return to San Felipe.

On the long level stretches, he mounted the burro and rode slowly. She didn't seem to mind his weight. He guided her with the makeshift cord reins. She responded easily, possibly glad to be carrying a lighter burden and without a bit in her mouth.

Diego often tried to put himself in the minds of animals, wondering what they were thinking or how they would react to certain situations. He had an affinity for creatures of all kinds. Domestic animals, especially, were subject to humans, and humans were the cruelest masters in the world—at least in his world. People did things out of hatred or spite or jealousy, or for no reason at all, whereas animals, unless rabid, did things for a reason—hunger, self-defense, protection of their young.

He took a deep breath of the fresh spring air and gazed at a yellow wash of flowers streaking the slope of a desert mountain a half-mile away. An hour later, the midafternoon sun lost much of its power when it was hidden by high mare's tails sweeping up from the west. With any luck, the sun would stay under cloud for a time because he had no hat and might suffer sunstroke after several hours unprotected from its full force. After working in the blacksmith shop, he considered himself conditioned to extreme heat, but the sun was a different matter.

Late in the afternoon, the fiery orb slid behind the mountain, replacing its rays with streaks of red and gold lancing high across the sky. Diego gazed in wonder at this display. Peace and silent beauty. When was the last time he'd felt like this? He couldn't remember. In the back of his mind was the thought that he must begin searching for a campsite and for water—practical things. But he put it off as the sunset lingered, and lingered. This display was only for him; he seemed alone in the universe.

The spectacular light show slowly began to fade, and he guided Lupida away from the plain hoofprints he was following and closer to the base of the western mountain, his gaze drifting upward, searching for some break in the wall of shattered rock.

It was then he noticed them—a half-dozen zopilotes wheeling a couple hundred feet above. As he watched, the black wings of the big Mexican buzzards were beginning to soar higher on the rising thermals as if they'd not expected their evening meal to be interrupted by a boy on a burro.

Diego was repelled by these creatures, but knew they had their place in nature. *Some dead animal out there,* he thought. But he wouldn't detour on their account; they would fly away at his approach.

He looked directly below where they circled. Were they going to fight over a kangaroo rat or some small rodent? It was probably something larger, like a javelina. He continued riding, wondering if Lupida would shy away from the smell of death.

An irregular shape lay on the ground. From this distance it looked too big for a wild hog. Perhaps a mule deer.

Out of curiosity, he rode closer. Then he saw it was a man. Within a few yards, he halted and slid off Lupida's back, tying the cord to a mesquite bush so she wouldn't wander away.

He stood off a distance for a minute to be sure the man was not pretending to be hurt so he could then jump up and rob him. There was no movement, and flies buzzed around him. There was no odor, so maybe he hadn't been dead long. He walked up boldly then, and squatted down, taking the man's shoulder and gently rolling him over.

His heart leapt into his mouth. He was staring into the face of Carlos Sandoval. He quickly put his fingers to the throat to feel for a pulse. Yes, he was alive; his heartbeat was not strong, but it was steady. Dried blood caked his shirt near the waist. The cotton shirt was stuck to the wound and he didn't want to pull it away for fear of starting the bleeding again. He took out his clasp knife and cut the cloth away so he could get an idea of the wound.

The soggy material came loose, and he saw what appeared to be a gunshot wound where a bullet had cut through the muscles in his side. He had no water, and saw no canteen nearby. There was also no mule or horse. Had the men who kidnapped the three gringos shot Sandoval and taken his mule? What had happened to the other two? Whatever had taken place, it had been only a few hours earlier.

He straightened up, and his arm bumped the nose of the burro, who had pulled her tether loose from the bush and come up behind him. *She must know her master,* he thought. The animal leaned down and nuzzled the chest of the unconscious man.

It was up to him to find water, and he gazed again at the rocky wall rising nearby. With the long days, he had at least two more hours of daylight. There was no danger from the sun now. Diego guessed Sandoval was unconscious from loss of blood and possibly heat stroke. But water was vital—for both of them and the burro—or they'd all become food for the zopilotes.

CHAPTER 23

Diego had to do something, and do it quickly, or Sandoval would die. Even if he had plenty of water, the wounded man might still die. There was no time to begin a search in the mountain for a seep or a tank.

He looked around for a barrel cactus. They sucked up moisture and retained it against extreme drought in order to survive. He mounted the burro so he could see a bit farther. There! He spotted three or four about fifty yards off. He got down and tied the burro more securely and jogged away, dodging among the creosote bushes, mesquite, and sage. His knife was his only tool, but it would have to do. He knelt by the cactus, which was about the shape and size of two large watermelons. Being careful not to prick his hands, he sliced off several rows of spines, and then dug into the green, waxy surface. Fluid leaked out and he tasted it. It would never replace lemonade, but it would keep them alive, if he could get enough of it. His knife blade was barely three inches long and he sliced long strips out of the soft interior. Stripping off his shirt, he used it like a leaky sack to fill it with the juicy pulp.

Dashing back, he knelt by the unconscious man and began to trickle the liquid onto his dry lips. No response. He turned Sandoval's head sideways so he wouldn't choke and squeezed some of the pulp into his mouth. After the fourth try, Sandoval gave a convulsive cough and his eyes fluttered open. He swallowed a time or two, and Diego squeezed another strip of the pulp into his mouth. He drank greedily, and signaled for another. He finished the six strips. "More!" he rasped.

"Wait. I'll cut some." Diego ran to the cactus and cut more pulp.

When he got back, Sandoval had pushed himself to a sitting position. His face was a mask of pain.

Diego handed him a slice of pulp to suck on. "Looks like you been shot."

"Bullet hit me in the back."

"That's good," the boy said. "Because there's a hole in front, too. It went through. And it's on your side, and the bleeding has stopped."

"A miracle," Sandoval said.

"You lost much blood."

Sandoval wrung out the stringy pulp.

"You remember me?"

Sandoval looked at him. "*Sí*. The boy from San Felipe." He glanced at the burro. "You have Lupida."

"Where is your mule?"

"With my friends, Charvein and Lucy." He licked his lips, and then winced. "Ahh! I think Satan himself is driving his pitchfork into me." He took another slice of pulp. "I was riding a horse I stole from the bandits," he continued. "When I passed out and fell off, he probably returned to his corral inside that mountain." He paused and glanced at the long twilight. "How long have I been here?"

"I do not know, *señor*. A few hours, *mas o menos*. I brought your burro and followed your trail to return her to you."

"*Gracias*, Diego."

Suddenly Sandoval's face changed. "I must signal my friends. They probably think I'm dead."

"How can you signal?"

"We arranged for me to fire three shots if I got into trouble and needed help." He reached for his Colt still held in place by the leather loop over its hammer.

"Will it not draw the bandits, too?" Diego asked.

"We'll have to chance it. I need help." He aimed his pistol in the general direction of the circling buzzards and fired off three blasts as quickly as he could cock the hammer and pull the trigger.

Diego took his hands from his ears as the echoes slammed back from the nearby mountain and were swallowed up in the desert stillness.

"Reach into my side pocket," Sandoval said, grimacing as he lowered the heavy pistol to his lap. "Give me those few loose cartridges."

Diego obeyed, being careful not to jar the wounded man.

Sandoval put the five shells on the ground beside him. "Now we wait to see if they heard my signal. Even so, it will take some time for them to get here. I'm so thirsty."

"I'll bring more of that cactus for you to chew."

"Gracias."

Diego made three more trips and cut into another barrel cactus, lugging back the dripping pulp in his shirt.

Dusk began to settle in as Sandoval sucked the juice. Finally he glanced at the darkening sky. "We'll try again." He fired the last three shots in the chambers, and then reloaded. "Do you have any matches for a fire?"

"No."

"I was hoping we could build a signal fire to help them find us." He took a deep breath. "I must tell you the danger you have put yourself in by saving my life." He went on to explain in detail what had happened. "So I don't think we are more than a mile from where those outlaws are smelting the gold and minting the coins. They might ride out here and kill us both."

"If we stay quiet, I do not think they can find us," Diego

said, noting that he could barely see Sandoval in the gathering darkness. There was no moon showing as yet. "Maybe it is a good thing we have no matches for a fire." He added this last as encouragement for Sandoval. Yet, he, himself, would have welcomed the warmth of a cheery blaze, regardless of the danger, since he was beginning to shiver without his shirt in the growing chill.

They continued to converse in low tones, and Diego related his own story.

"Ahh, one man's misfortune is another man's blessing," Sandoval murmured. "Divine Providence has brought you and my burro to me."

"You could still die," Diego blurted out before he thought. *What a stupid thing to say!*

But Sandoval only chuckled softly. "No, my friend, I feel confident God did not bring you all this way, and help you revive me only to let me die. I have been through much worse than this. As you grow older, you will outlive many hardships and disappointments, but they will make you stronger and wiser."

"Ha! You sound like one of the old men in the village."

"Es verdad."

They fell silent for a time. The only sounds were the howl of a coyote in the distance as the moon appeared from behind the mountain. Lupida raised her head from browsing on some mesquite leaves, but then resumed.

Another hour passed, and suddenly Sandoval, whose head was drooping, sat up straight. "Did you hear that?"

"What?" Diego had shivered himself warm and was dozing.

"Listen!"

Diego strained his hearing. Nothing.

"I heard a horseshoe strike a rock," Sandoval said. "There is no other sound like it." He raised the Colt from his lap.

Diego knew the wounded man dared not fire the three-shot signal again in case the riders coming toward them were not friendly. He sat still, holding his breath.

The moon was still nearly full and flooded its light down on them. Diego strained to see and could suddenly make out movement. It was two riders, and there was a third horse. No! Against the slight paleness of the night sky behind the riders, he saw the longer ears of a mule.

Before he could whisper to Sandoval, Lupida raised her head. *HEE HAW!* The deafening bray announced the arrival of visitors.

There was a scuffle of horses moving, and then a shout, "Sandoval?"

"Over here!" Diego shouted.

Sandoval tried to yell, but his voice was only a croak.

"I told you it was not my time to die," Sandoval said to Diego, as Lucy and Charvein rode up and dismounted.

CHAPTER 24

"You're a very lucky man." Charvein helped ease Sandoval onto his side. A blazing fire provided plenty of light for him to see both entry and exit wounds. He used canteen water to gently clean the dried blood.

"Luck has always been my *compadre*." Sandoval grimaced as Charvein poured a little tequila on the wound.

"Where'd you get that?" Lucy asked.

"Always keep a bottle in my saddlebags," Charvein grinned. "For snakebite. I hate the taste of the stuff, but it's cheap. It's even good for starting fires with damp wood."

Lucy had a pot of coffee on the fire, and was soaking some jerky to make a broth.

"Now that most of the blood's cleaned off, it doesn't look too bad," Charvein said, ripping up his clean, spare shirt for a bandage. "Looks like it just clipped the muscle along your side and didn't penetrate the abdominal cavity. You have a gash on your head that will be sore for a while, too," he added.

"Must've hit my head on something when I passed out and fell off the horse," Sandoval said, touching his scalp just above the hairline.

"Your hair's all matted. I'll clean it up in a minute." Charvein finished wrapping and snugging up the bandage around the small man's midsection.

Both Diego and Sandoval had taken long drinks from the canteens, and Lucy had given Diego a spare shirt from her saddlebags. It came close to fitting him.

"Ah, that's beginning to feel better," Sandoval sighed, leaning back against a saddle and sipping the scalding coffee laced with sugar.

"I think you've lost more blood than you can afford," Charvein said, noting that the firelight couldn't quite erase the paleness showing under his friend's dark skin. "You'll need rest, food, and medical attention."

"I can ride," Sandoval said.

"And take a chance on that wound opening up? Not for a while, you won't."

Charvein poured himself some coffee and sat down, cross-legged, on his ground cover. "Okay, I want to hear the stories from both of you," he said, looking from Diego to Sandoval.

Diego first filled them in on how he came to be there with the burro.

"Thank God for your nasty boss," Charvein remarked.

Then Sandoval gave his account. "Was that only twenty-four hours ago?" he finished. "How long was I out?"

"Yes. It was midnight when we last saw you."

Sandoval glanced out into the dark. "With this big campfire, shouldn't we have someone stand watch? We couldn't be more than a mile or so from Flynn and his men."

"We're safe enough," Charvein said. "We heard a lot of shooting, and then nothing for several hours. When you didn't show up by daylight, we waited all day until dusk and then started back to look for you."

"They were all gone," Lucy said.

"Gone?"

"Yes, cleared out," Charvein said. "The fires had burned down, but the men, the smelter, the horses, the wagon—all vanished. We thought you were dead or had been taken captive. We were looking around to see if they'd left anything, hoping

177

we wouldn't find your body. Then we heard your shots."

"But the echoes bounce around in these hills, and we couldn't make out exactly where the shots came from," Lucy added.

"We were looking on the other side of the pass when you fired again," Charvein said, "and then we were able to draw a bead on you."

"That's probably the last we'll see of Flynn and his Border Brigands," Sandoval said, using the name the newspapers had begun calling the gang. "But at least I got the evidence we needed." With an effort, he slid a hand into his pocket and drew out the ornate gold necklace.

Charvein took it, examining the delicate work. The gold glowed in the firelight. It appeared three stones had been pried from their mountings as the piece was being prepared for melting. "Good work. But you paid a stiff price for it." He handed the necklace to Lucy. "We'll have to identify it from the bills of lading, but I have no doubt it's a piece from one of the robberies. Too bad I don't still have that Webley pistol as another piece of evidence."

"At least we know who did it, but we still don't know why," Sandoval said. "It probably doesn't matter much now that they're long gone and will never be charged with the crime."

Charvein was thoughtful. "They may be gone from here, but that doesn't mean they'll no longer be sending masked gunmen north of the border to rob Wells Fargo. Maybe since their hideout had been discovered, they knew they'd never be secure here, so they pulled up stakes and headed deeper into the wilderness. I noticed their wagon was very sturdy. It was built to carry a lot of weight. Did that smelter look like it was portable?"

Sandoval nodded. "*Sí.* It was not large."

"And they had at least a dozen horses. There was nothing I saw there that couldn't be moved."

The jerky had boiled for several minutes and Lucy poured

out a half cup of the thin broth and handed it to Sandoval. "We need some real food," she said. "They did not leave any steaks or bread behind. Only a pile of bones from various cuts of meat and some other garbage."

"I have a half loaf of bread left from what Flynn gave us," Charvein said. "Maybe I can get a jackrabbit with my rifle."

"We still have a good supply of jerky," Lucy said. "And we ate only a little of that bacon Flynn gave us."

"Enough to make it back to the border if we eat light," Charvein said.

"Where do you think the Border Brigands have gone?" Sandoval asked.

"The tracks of a heavy wagon and many horses lead straight out toward the southwest."

"What's in that direction? The Sierra Madre?" Lucy asked.

"No," Diego replied. "The mountains and deep barrancas of the Sierra Madre are far to the east. That is where the Tarahumara Indians live. The men in the village say it is very rough country."

"To the south and west is the Sea of Cortez," Sandoval said.

"If they go many miles that direction, they'll be too far to make any convenient raids across the border," Charvein said.

They sat quietly for a minute or two. Charvein got up to make sure the two horses, mule, and burro were securely hobbled. Then he came back and added a few dry sticks to the fire. "What are your plans, Diego? Return to San Felipe?"

"Never. I would like to ride with you back to the border and stay in the United States."

Charvein absorbed this. "You have been a lifesaver for us. And you could help even more by making sure Sandoval and Lucy reach one of the American border settlements."

"Where are *you* going?" Lucy asked.

"Our job is only half done. We know who the robbers are, but we've only flushed them. They're still on the loose."

"We could send a telegraph message to the Mexican authorities when we get back, so the *Federales* can hunt them," Lucy suggested.

"They've probably been careful to obey the law in Mexico," Charvein said. "Our government could only ask for cooperation and extradition. A very long shot, fraught with politics and delays. Coughlin did not want to blow this all out of proportion and put himself and Wells Fargo in the stage lights."

"Are you suggesting you go after them alone?" Sandoval asked.

"A scouting party of one," Charvein said. "They can't travel fast with that livestock and a heavy wagon. Their trail is plain. I could catch up quickly and harass them with hit and run raids."

"What will that accomplish?"

"Maybe nothing, but it would let them know they aren't getting away clean. There will be consequences for their robberies. And I can find out where they're headed."

Lucy's face plainly showed her anguish at this plan. But she said nothing—only looked down and busied herself checking the amount of coffee left in the pot.

The fire was burning down, falling in on itself. Diego crept closer, wrapping his arms around himself.

"Well, what do you think?" Charvein asked when nobody spoke.

"Very risky," Sandoval said. "If you didn't return, we would never know what happened to you."

Charvein brushed aside this objection with a wave of his hand. "The main question is, do you feel you can make it back to the border with the help of these two?"

"You know me by now," Sandoval said. "I will endure like a redwood after a forest fire—this will only make me come back stronger."

"How's the broken arm?"

"No worse than before. I'll make it. Diego saved my life and Lucy and I have been through a lot together."

"All right, then, it's decided. I'll take a little jerky, two canteens of water, my rifle and shells. I can hunt along the way. If I see I can't do it for some reason, I'll break off and head for the border."

"Don't wait too long to decide," Sandoval said. "There is a lot of barren desert out there."

"There are many plants and small animals. I will survive. I just want to bring down Flynn and his boys."

"Probably only two or three hours until daylight." Charvein stood up and stretched. "We all need some sleep badly. No need to stand watch. Everything will look brighter after we're rested."

He turned to the boy. "Diego, I can't thank you enough. You're the only able-bodied man in this threesome, so I'm counting on you. Take Sandoval's rifle since he can't use it. He still has his Colt and a few shells for emergencies. Lucy has her .38, so you should be able to protect yourselves. I'd advise you to rest here tomorrow and then start out tomorrow night so you can travel by moonlight. Cooler and safer. There are still Apaches and Mexican bandits roaming Sonora."

He pulled a blanket from his bedroll and tossed it to Diego. "One thing more," he said to them. "Don't wire Wells Fargo when you get to the first telegraph office across the line. Our friendly telegrapher in Yuma will pick up on it and try to have you eliminated before you can get back. I have forty dollars here to spare; I'll keep eleven. And Lucy has some money. If you must, hire some help to reach the railroad and buy one-way tickets to Yuma. Don't talk to anyone along the way. Report directly to Barton Coughlin at the Wells Fargo office." He turned to Sandoval. "See if you can find a doctor to look at that

181

wound before you do all that. Or get some food and help at a mine or ranch."

Charvein felt he was laying a lot on them, injured and hungry as they were. But they had a horse, a mule, a burro, all in good condition, a little food and water, and three guns. He was confident that Sandoval, weak as he was, could ride slowly without harm after a day's rest. Lucy had courage and good judgment. She'd been tough enough to cross much of the Sonoran Desert alone to warn them. The malnourished boy, Diego, wise beyond his years and familiar with the country, would be a great help. The three of them, barring Apaches, bandits, or accidents, could make the ride through arid country to the border in roughly two days.

About his own mission, he was not so certain.

Chapter 25

Even though Charvein was eager to start while the trail was fresh, he forced himself to get a good night's sleep.

He awoke before light and poked up the fire while Sandoval and Diego still slept. Lucy stirred and sat up, brushing the hair out of her eyes.

"I'm going hunting," he said, noting she was pretty, even in the early morning firelight. "Just through the pass," he pointed, "and over yonder near that stream. Probably be gone most of the morning. If you hear shots, don't be alarmed, unless there are more than two or three. I'll be back as soon as possible."

He saddled up quickly as she was pouring canteen water into the coffeepot.

Riding along the flank of the mountain, he looked carefully in the dim light until he found the almost hidden entrance to the narrow passage. It was still dark inside the mountain as his horse's shod hooves clattered along inside the rocky cleft. Dismounting near the end of the roofless tunnel, he led his horse, rifle in hand, to scout ahead. The clearing was still deserted.

Then, riding quickly across the cove, he went another mile, dismounted, left his horse on a long tether fastened to a picket pin, and trotted on foot with his loaded Winchester.

Hiding in a thicket near the stream, he settled down to wait. Small birds were flitting in the underbrush, their chirping the only sound greeting the day. If he stayed quiet, they wouldn't give away his presence.

Twenty minutes later, he caught a slight movement from the corner of his eye, and barely turning his head, saw a mule deer approaching silently to drink on the opposite bank of the flowing stream. It would be a shot of fifty yards.

"Oh, my God, you're a lifesaver!" Lucy cried when Charvein rode up with the mule deer across his saddle. It was only then that Charvein realized how worried she'd been about the prospect of no food.

Diego helped field-dress the carcass, cutting much of the meat into strips for drying and smoking on the campfire.

They satisfied their hunger with juicy venison steaks grilled on sticks over the open fire. Hardly a word was said as they ate their fill. This was probably the best medical treatment Sandoval could have had, Charvein thought.

"Ahh, manna from heaven," Sandoval sighed, wiping his fingers on a sprig of mesquite leaves.

"The Israelites didn't have to shoot their manna," Charvein observed.

"Weren't some rams caught in the bushes by their horns so the Jews could have meat?" Sandoval asked, arching his brows.

"You got me there," Charvein admitted. "I guess the Lord provided because they didn't have Winchesters."

He got up and stretched, pondering how much farther away Flynn and his gang of robbers were traveling each hour that he dawdled. He had to get going.

But, then, as he saddled his horse, a thought occurred to him. They would be moving cross-country only as fast as a horse could walk. The two- or four-horse hitches pulling that loaded wagon in the heat, through sand and washouts, detouring around obstacles and low mountains, would certainly slow them. The teams would have to be changed at least every eight to ten miles, delaying them further. And they would certainly stop and camp overnight.

He began to feel more confident that, traveling at a steady pace, he could come close to catching up before darkness overtook him tonight. Even so, he had to move out now. He checked his rifle and made sure he had more than a hundred extra rounds. He shoved the remaining half-pound of burlap-wrapped bacon into his greasy saddlebags, knowing it would melt down to lean in a day. He took two cooked steaks and wrapped them in the burlap as well. The rest of the deer and remaining bread, he'd leave for them. What meat they couldn't eat today and smoke to preserve, they'd cook and carry to eat before it spoiled. He had divided their remaining wax-coated matches and kept a dozen for himself.

Lucy stepped up to him as he tugged down his hat brim and prepared to mount.

"I don't have a good feeling about this," she said, softly.

"You'll be all right." He looked down into her eyes. "You can make the border in two easy days. Just be sure Sandoval doesn't jar that wound and break it open. If he gets too weak, just stop and rest a few hours. But don't skyline yourselves. Travel at night if you have a moon."

"I'm talking about you."

"I'll play whatever I'm dealt. Not taking any chances. I'm no hero. Just want to see if I can get this job done as long as we've come this far."

She stood there, her hand on his arm.

He reached to tug on the saddle girth, though he'd already tightened it.

Then, impulsively, he took her in his arms and kissed her.

She locked her arms around his neck for several long seconds.

Then she stepped back, and without another word, turned away.

Charvein swung into the saddle, and turned his horse. "I'm depending on you three to help each other," he said. "I'll see you in Yuma in a week or two."

The sun had not yet peeked over the rim of the distant mountains when he cantered away.

He retraced his route of that morning, picked up the obvious trail of the wagon and dozen horses, and kept going. He trotted his horse for a while, then walked him for a half mile, then cantered. Every hour, he dismounted and rested for ten minutes before starting again. He wondered if Flynn knew where he was going. Surely, he had some destination in mind.

Hour after hour he followed the tracks to the southwest. The Sea of Cortez was to the southwest. But how far? Then he recalled he still had his compass in the saddlebags if he needed it.

In midafternoon, his mind wandered back to Lucy. He'd kissed her on impulse, without thinking. What were his real feelings for her? They'd been through much together in the past year or so. He'd saved her life from kidnappers and later she'd saved his from a man about to knife him in his sleep. He'd seen her progress from a dreamy girl, ruled by her imagination of a romantic past in literature, to one honed by hardship, who gazed on reality with calm confidence. Was she thinking of marriage? They'd become old friends in a rather short time. She *was* young and attractive, but he didn't want to confuse shared hardship and friendship with love.

On the other hand, what did she see in him? In his early forties, he was at least eight to ten years her senior, and pushing on toward middle age. Until he'd taken this current job with Wells Fargo, his economic future seemed dim and uncertain. But he liked what he was doing now, even when the job was routine. Wells Fargo seemed to be a company that would endure. It had survived the transition from staging to railroads, from courier service to banking. No one could see the future, but he thought he'd stick with this job and see where it led him with the company.

He thrust the thought from his mind. Letting their relationship evolve would be the best thing to do. But, if he decided to marry and settle down to family life, he'd better do it soon while he was still young enough.

The trail he was following went on and on into the distance. In early afternoon he saw where they had paused and the tracks milled around. Probably a stop to rest the draft animals. There was no water anywhere about, so he assumed they carried barrels of fresh water on the wagon. He, too, reined up and dismounted, loosening the saddle, and slipping the bit from his horse's mouth, letting him drink a hatful of water—probably not enough, but all he could spare from his two canteens.

Flynn's party was still out there ahead someplace beyond the horizon. Charvein had left behind the low desert mountains. The terrain ahead appeared to be drier and flatter, covered with regularly spaced mesquite and low desert shrubs as far as he could see. To his right front, miles away, rose a peak, blue-gray in the distance. He estimated its height to be about 4,000 feet. He consulted his map. Probably Cerro del Pinacate, he guessed. But his route lay to the south of that, straight into the Desierto del Altar that stretched ahead for roughly 150 miles clear to the Colorado River. If his quarry was carrying their own water, they must have a lot of it on board the wagon to be able to cross this wasteland.

But then, squinting into the glare from under his hat brim, he decided maybe they were not trying to cross it. The trail seemed to be angling south toward the gulf.

He scrubbed a calloused hand across the stubble on his sunburned cheeks. Should he attempt to stay after them? He would run out of water very soon and would have to turn back.

He must ration what water he had for his horse; a man afoot out here would not survive more than a day or two.

Maybe if he slowed his pace, he would last longer. He decided to stop where he was, in the meager shade of the paloverde, and wait out the hottest part of the day, and then start out near sunset. He pulled off the saddle and blanket and let his horse roll in the dry sandy soil. Then he tied the animal on a long tether, and spread out his ground cover to rest in the shade.

He dozed off and on for three hours, then got up, saddled, and started again, hat brim pulled down against the westering sun. Within an hour, high clouds slid up from the southwest, covering the sun, and providing relief.

The tracks continued to the southwest, and Charvein stopped twice to scan the distance ahead with the field glasses he'd taken back from Sandoval. He had to be careful he didn't run upon them too quickly. Any of them watching their back trail could spot a lone rider a long way off in this open desert.

A long twilight stretched the day. He walked his horse into the dusk. The wind picked up, pushing ahead the lowering clouds and hastening darkness. Dust and fine sand irritated his eyes, making it even harder to see the wagon tracks. This would be a very black night with no moon to guide him.

When darkness closed down, he selected a spot to camp near a thick stand of mesquite. He probably could have started a small fire without being seen, but decided not to. Even a speck of light in total darkness could be seen for a great distance.

He dug out one of the cooked steaks and gnawed the delicious meat from it. He'd save the other one for tomorrow. It should still be good.

A flash of lightning revealed a high thunderhead to the west. Occasional spring cloudbursts still watered this land. Only recently had the primrose, the mariposa lily, the night blooming hedgehog, and the brittlebush shed their colorful flowers to prepare for the long summer.

A few minutes later another flash was followed within seconds by a booming crash of thunder, warning him the storm was close. His horse sidled nervously. Charvein tied the tether more securely to the base of a thick-limbed mesquite bush.

He covered his saddle on the ground with the slicker to keep it dry, then inhaled deeply of the smell of desert sage and the dampness of the oncoming rain. He took off his hat and slipped his head through the hole in the tightly woven poncho. He didn't care how wet he got; this would be a wondrous relief.

During the height of the booming thunder and lightning show, Charvein threw his own blanket over his horse's head and held onto his bridle to keep him relatively calm while the rain sluiced down in sheets, blowing sideways.

The storm moved off to the east about four in the morning and Charvein was able to doze off and on until nearly daylight.

Refreshed, but soggy and tired, he felt washed clean of sweat and dust. As soon as it was light enough to see, he led his horse to a rivulet of water running down a desert wash so he could drink his fill. Charvein wished he had a bag of oats for the animal, but "if wishes were horses, beggars would ride" as the old saying went. He filled both two-quart canteens with the reddish brown water, knowing the silt would settle later so he could drink. He hunted for—but failed to find—any cleaner water to drink; muddy rainwater and beef jerky constituted breakfast. There was no brush or wood dry enough to start a campfire and cook a little bacon.

At least his saddle was dry, he thought, as he mounted up and began to scout for the trail of the wagon and horses.

But they were gone—washed out as if they'd never existed.

Chapter 26

He crisscrossed the route he'd been riding, just to make sure he hadn't missed it. Perhaps there was a deeper, water-filled rut made by the wagon that still showed the way. But if any such thing existed, he was unable to find it.

He reined up and leaned forward on the saddle horn, staring off into the distance. What now? The mountain peak was still in the same relative position to the north and west of him. He pulled the map from the saddlebag and studied it. If Flynn had continued on the same route, he would reach the Gulf of California, or the Sea of Cortez as it was known. The map showed a village there—Puerto Peñaso—probably not over thirty miles in a direct line from where he sat. Charvein thought for a long minute or two. It would seem logical, traveling with a heavy wagon and a dozen horses, they would go there. Why would they try to cross the wide desert to the Colorado River— unless they were planning to go upriver to Yuma? When they left their hideout, Flynn could not have anticipated they'd be blessed with plenty of water from a storm that would allow them to refill their water barrels to see them all the way across the *Gran Desierto* to the Colorado. Maybe they knew of some source of water he didn't know about.

No, chances are they were headed for the gulf, if for no other reason than to resupply. Even if that wasn't their destination, Charvein decided to break off the chase and head there himself. He had to have supplies and also feed for his horse in order to ride north to the border and home.

Once the decision was made, he rode on in the fresh morning breathing deeply of fragrant desert air scrubbed clean by the rain. The sun rose overhead and began to suck up the humidity. By noon he was perspiring freely, but two hours later he was dried off and comfortable.

By late afternoon, tired and hungry, he spotted some marshy ground ahead. The westerly breeze brought the smell of saltwater. Riding up to the tall grass and cattails, he identified this as the small delta of Sonoita Creek.

His horse took a long drink of the fresh water, and then Charvein moved on, knowing the village was less than five miles farther.

At sundown he rode into the muddy streets of Puerto Peñasco. A pier thrust out into the water with several good-sized fishing boats moored to each side. Smaller skiffs were drawn up on the beach, two or three fishermen tending them. There was no sign of extra horses, or the wagon he sought. Several Mexican pedestrians were going about their business in the quiet evening. Three or four children were running along the beach with a dog.

Although he half expected this might be a port for American travelers to try their luck at saltwater fishing, he saw no white faces anywhere. Flynn and his men were not in evidence. Somehow they had eluded him and gone elsewhere. Maybe Flynn had another hideout somewhere away from here. This sleepy village looked to be even smaller than San Felipe.

After a careful look around, he rode up to a two-story hotel and dismounted stiffly. He'd get himself a room for the night and have his horse stabled and taken care of. Then he'd resupply at some store in the morning and be on his way home. He dismounted at the hitching rail of the hotel and pulled out his map. It might be quicker if he followed the road that skirted the edge of the Sea of Cortez to the Gulf of Santa Clara, and then traded his horse and saddle for a ticket on the twice-weekly sternwheeler that steamed between Yuma and the gulf on the Colorado River. But then he recalled he'd rented the horse and rig. They weren't his to sell or trade. But likely the boat had stalls on the main deck to accommodate his animal.

He checked into the hotel using his meager knowledge of Spanish and the clerk's better knowledge of English. It would feel good to clean up and shave and sleep in a bed, even if this place looked as though it might have its share of bedbugs. He was in a tropic area. Even scorpions and such annoyances probably survived the winter here.

But first, he'd see to the care of his horse who'd carried him so far these last few days. He signed the register and laid down two silver dollars, inquired about the location of the livery, and walked back outside.

A hundred yards down the street, he found the livery and a Mexican sitting outside on a stool in the deepening dusk, whittling and nursing a jar half full of some beverage. The dying sun cast a red sheen on the calm waters of the gulf giving the village one last burst of reflected light. Coal oil lamps were sparking up at intervals like lightning bugs in windows and the two saloons he could see.

Mosquitoes hummed around Charvein's ears while he negotiated in halting Spanish with the owner for overnight care of his horse. He handed the Mexican the reins and a silver dollar. American cartwheels were as readily accepted here as silver pesos.

Stripping off the saddlebags, he threw them over a shoulder and pulled his Winchester from its sheath.

Only then did he realize how fatigued he was. Food and sleep would set him right again.

He walked out into the humid dusk, breathing faint odors of

fish and mildew. How unlike this coastal village was compared to the arid desert he'd just crossed.

Turning back toward the hotel in the deepening twilight, he caught his toe on a wagon tongue that protruded from a narrow space between two buildings. Muttering a curse, he glanced up. What idiot had left a wagon parked here? He glanced into the deep shadows . . . and froze. Looking casually about to be sure no pedestrians were nearby, he stepped into the alley to take a closer look. It was a Studebaker wagon, not overly large, but heavily built with thick braces, a deep bed, and wider than usual ironbanded wheel rims. A narrow green stripe was painted down each side, ending in a curly flair on the tailgate. Damp sand still clung to the wheels. His heart began to pound. No doubt about it—this was the wagon he'd seen at Flynn's hideout and had been tracking across the desert.

He stepped up onto a wheel spoke and looked inside. Empty. The portable smelter and all supplies and tools were gone. Offloaded where? To some building in town for storage? Or did Flynn own a place he operated from on the gulf? But how could it be found? He wondered briefly if any of Flynn's men were putting up at the hotel. It appeared to be the only hostelry in the small village.

He stepped back around to the livery entrance. It was nearly full dark now and he called out, "Anybody here?"

A match flared and the little Mexican owner lighted a coal oil lamp, set the chimney back in place, and hung the lamp on a nail just inside the door.

"Do you know who owns that wagon parked around the corner next to this livery?"

The man's brown eyes regarded him blankly with no hint of understanding.

"The wagon. Where's the man who belongs to that wagon?" He stepped back and pointed at the nearly invisible wagon tongue that thrust out onto the boardwalk.

The man shook his head. *"No comprende, señor."*

"I'll bet," Charvein muttered to himself, shaking his head and walking away. "Likely took a hefty tip to say that." Perhaps the hotel clerk would know. He seemed to have a command of English.

By the light of the lantern, Charvein could see that nearly every stall in the livery was occupied. The man must do a good business. Or . . . could these be the horses owned by Flynn's gang? Charvein had not looked closely enough at them earlier to know.

At the hotel desk he inquired about the wagon. The lean clerk rubbed his slim black mustache as if in deep thought. "We have many wagons in town," he said.

"Did several men ride in here today or yesterday? They would have had a wagon with them, and several horses."

"Many *hombres* ride into Puerto Peñasco every day," he replied quickly—too quickly, Charvein thought.

The clerk shrugged. "They come to fish or wait for the boat that comes from Yuma and goes down the Baja to California." He made a circle in the air to show how the boat looped around the peninsula.

"Gracias," Charvein nodded, knowing he would get nothing from this man. He walked away toward the adjacent café, carrying his saddlebags and rifle. He would pursue this in the morning. Flynn and his men had gone to ground someplace close by for the night.

He ordered scrambled eggs and refried beans with coffee.

The food was good, but the coffee was the worst he'd ever drunk. It tasted like a dead cigar that'd been relighted for the third time. He didn't know if it was the water, or the thick, gamey goat's milk he'd added that might have gone sour. But he ordered a beer to take the taste out of his mouth.

He nursed the beer and sat staring at the gulf two hundred yards down the slope. Large shutters opening onto a veranda were swung up and propped open to the balmy night air, admitting an onslaught of buzzing insects. The sound of waves washing up onto the beach added to the sleepy evening. The quiet, rhythmic swish of water told him the tide was probably receding. Barely visible against the lighter background of sky were the masts of several fishing boats and superstructures of a few small steamers that were tied up to both sides of a long pier that extended out far enough to provide deep water, even at low tide.

He tipped up his glass and drained the beer.

The glass thumped abruptly to the wooden table as an idea suddenly dawned on him and he leaned forward to stare harder out toward the small harbor. The boats! Of course. That made sense. Flynn would have a mobile base of operations. He'd been able to pull out of the mountain hideout within a few hours with wagon and horses. Why not have a boat here, from where he could operate and still be ready to cast off at a moment's notice if threatened? He could have sold or traded the horses. And the wagon was stored beside the livery for later use.

Tired as he was, the bed could wait. He had to have a look tonight, or he'd never get to sleep.

He put a silver dollar on the table for his meal and headed out the door, carrying the rifle and saddlebags.

A gibbous moon had risen over the nearby trees that shaded the village. It gave just enough light to make out a few details of each boat he passed. Flying insects buzzed around coal oil lanterns that hung from posts along the pier twenty feet apart, giving enough light to see where he was walking.

There was no one on the long pier at the moment and he made his way slowly, scrutinizing each boat as he passed. Most were obviously local fishing vessels between twenty and thirty feet in length designed to take on deeper, rougher water. But he counted three steamers, plus another, larger one, anchored thirty yards offshore. Of those at the pier, only one was moored with its rakish bow facing seaward. He paused and took a longer look. The vessel was about fifty feet in length with a stern paddlewheel. The boat was large enough for coastal cruising, but small enough for shallow rivers and inlets. He suspected it was V-bottomed with a keel of some kind. It would take a crew of at least four, but had room for several more as passengers. The depth of hull could carry a small cargo. It was painted green, like the stripe on the wagon.

He wondered if anyone was aboard. It was too early for most people to be in bed. He hesitated only a few seconds. The owner or the crew must be ashore. He had to have a look inside.

Glancing around, he found himself alone on the pier. Quickly he put a leg over the cap rail and slid onto the main deck, being careful not to bang his rifle against anything.

Through an overhead window of the pilothouse he could see the top half of the wheel spokes. Slipping quietly aft, he tried the handle of the first door he came to. Locked—as was the next one. If anyone was inside, the watertight doors would prevent even a sliver of light from escaping around the edges. He crept back to the paddlewheel at the stern and crossed over to the starboard side. As he turned to go forward, he saw a small circle of light dimly glowing through an opaque curtain in a porthole. He held his carbine in his right hand and gripped the door handle with his left, pressing down slowly. A muted click and the latch released. He took a deep breath and yanked the door open, swinging the rifle up.

"Come in and put the gun down," Flynn's voice said.

Charvein squinted against the sudden light. He stepped over the sill holding his carbine level.

Flynn sat in a swivel chair by a tiny wooden desk. "I was

expecting you." He was not wearing a belt gun.

Charvein was taken aback for a split second but quickly recovered. His eyes darted around the small cabin, expecting a trap. But the two of them were alone in what appeared to be the captain's quarters, furnished with a bunk, tiny writing desk, two chairs, and a few books and charts in a small bookcase. A gimbaled overhead oil lamp cast yellow light. With one hand he reached to pull the heavy door shut behind him. "Get up!" Charvein commanded. "You're under arrest for possession of stolen gold. We'll get to the armed robbery later."

Flynn chuckled and didn't move. "You're a persistent devil, I'll give you that. I almost wish you were on my team."

"I said to move." Charvein gestured with the carbine. "You're coming back to Yuma to face charges."

Charvein heard the door start to open behind him. He jumped to the side, swinging the gun barrel down and jacking a shell into the chamber. He caught a glimpse of the rough-looking Logan and the glint of a pistol. Charvein fired from the hip. The bullet struck the metal door lever, ricocheting into the man's gun hand.

Logan yelled and dodged back, kicking the door shut.

Something slammed Charvein from behind and he hit the deck with Flynn on his back. As he went down he felt a sharp blow to his abdomen when he landed on the tilted edge of the rifle stock. For a second or two he was paralyzed with pain.

Flynn gave him a rabbit punch to the back of the neck, and lights spangled before his eyes. Stunned by both blows, he was vaguely aware of Flynn wrenching the Winchester from under them.

His blurred vision began to clear as Flynn yanked him over onto his back and raised the rifle butt to smash him. Instantly reacting, Charvein coiled into a ball, both knees to his chest, and kicked out hard. One bootheel caught Flynn square in the face. With a strangled cry, the outlaw dropped the carbine and fell back, blood gushing from his nose.

Gasping, Charvein rolled to his feet. He lunged for the carbine, but a boot came out of nowhere and kicked it into a corner. Then his arms were pinned from behind with a grip like a gorilla. "Hold it right there, mister!" a rough voice said. Charvein was powerless in the grip and heard another man coming into the room.

Charvein looked at Flynn who was struggling to his feet, eyes streaming tears and blood dripping from his nose onto his white shirt.

He suddenly regretted his decision to come aboard.

Chapter 27

"Shall we throw him over the side?" the rough voice asked.

Flynn shook his head and pointed to a chair. "Search him for weapons and then put him there," he said in a choked voice.

While the big man held Charvein, the second man went over him quickly.

"He's clean."

Charvein was thrown into a wooden armchair, and for the first time saw his two attackers. Both were strangers to him. The man who'd held him was roughly six-two and two-hundred twenty pounds. The other was five-ten or so, with brown hair and mustache. He was covering Charvein with his own Winchester.

"You want we should tie him to that chair?"

"That won't be necessary." Flynn held a stained bandanna to his nose, and wiped the blood from his lip. "Bring us two beers from the galley. We're going to have a talk." He opened a drawer in the desk and drew out the Webley-Pryse revolver Charvein recognized. He had no doubt it was loaded.

"While you're at it," Flynn said as he took the Winchester and the men began to leave the cabin, "I could use a towel and some water."

The two men left the door standing open.

"Damned shame it had to come to this." Flynn seated himself on the corner of the small desk. "You probably broke my nose, and I'll have to go to a doctor and have it straightened before I can face the world again."

It stood to reason a man as handsome as Flynn would be more worried about his looks than anything else. "Face" said nothing further but continued holding the bandanna to his nose until the bleeding had nearly stopped.

By then the big man reappeared with two foamy mugs of beer. Apparently they had kegs stowed in the galley.

The smaller man came in with a tin pan of water and a hand towel and set them on the desk. "Need anything else, Boss?" he asked as he turned to leave.

"No. But leave the door open to get some air in here." Flynn stood up. "Did Logan take a slug?"

"Yeah. He's in there cussin'. Took the tip off his third finger, but he'll be okay."

"Hmmm . . . Okay. Stay close by, in case I need you."

"Yessir."

The pair disappeared and Flynn spent the next several minutes cleansing the blood from his damaged face. The bridge of his nose was red and swollen. It was also slightly bent.

Charvein noticed Flynn was not entirely ignoring him while he worked, and was careful to keep both the pistol and carbine close at hand.

Charvein sipped his beer and assessed his chances of getting away. It was about eight or nine feet across the cabin to the outlaw boss—too far to make a leap for him without getting himself shot. Besides, as he breathed and pressed a hand to his side, he began to wonder at the pain. He might have done himself some internal damage when he fell on the edge of the walnut stock with Flynn's weight on his back.

Finally, Flynn put the towel down and took up his beer.

"Well, Mister Marc Charvein, we meet again. You're as hard to get rid of as a case of scabies." He carefully wiped foam from his upper lip, and set his mug down on the desk. "I'm afraid you're going to regret not taking my hospitality and going on about your business." He pulled up the swivel chair and seated himself. The Winchester carbine rested on the desk.

"You *are* my business," Charvein replied.

Flynn smiled grimly. "We figured you wouldn't let well enough alone, and would make some further attempt to interfere. It was no trouble for my men to spot you as soon as you came in sight of the village. If you didn't happen to find us before we left in the morning, all would be well. But since you were persistent enough to discover our wagon, and now the boat, we'll have to deal with you."

Charvein wondered why they didn't just shoot him and be done with it, but he kept silent, not wanting to put any ideas into the man's head.

"Since you've come this far and gone to so much trouble to track me down, I feel you've probably earned an explanation." He picked up the pistol and placed it in his lap. "This is just a reminder not to make any sudden moves, even if you think I've become careless and inattentive." He smiled again with his mouth only while his blue eyes remained hard as sapphires.

Charvein almost regretted breaking Flynn's nose. Wounded pride in a vain man would surely bring down torture or death at the end of this conversation. He had a sinking feeling he would never get off this boat alive.

"I'm sure you and your friends and your bosses at Wells Fargo think that we are just another band of highwaymen bent on enriching ourselves at others' expense—common vermin to be exterminated from decent society."

Charvein did not reply.

"Nothing could be further from the truth. You've probably noticed a pattern. Most of what my men take from the express car is consigned by a man named Adolphus Grindell."

"Figured there was a connection," Charvein said.

"Yes, in their excitement and rush, my men have picked up a few other things—regretfully. But they are human and make mistakes." He took a swallow of his beer.

"Adolph and I have known each other for several years. In fact, we were once partners. We're nothing alike, but we had one thing in common—we were both dead broke and trying to 'strike it rich' as westerners say. And, by heaven, we did! It took us many months of prospecting and living on nearly nothing, but we stumbled onto a vein of rich ore in the Stillwater Range of Nevada, near Carson Sink. A remote hell that nobody had really explored until we got there. You might know it as the Alhambra. Exotic sounding, isn't it? Well, when we registered our joint claim, it was simply called the Badger Mine, because it was that feisty little critter who led us to it. I think he has another mine now he calls Halloran's Luck, named after an employee who discovered it for him.

"But never mind the details of all that. Things went along well for a time, and we began to take out richer and richer ore. We had signed an agreement to split all profits evenly. I finally reached the point where I felt I could propose to a lovely girl I had met in North Carolina. I told Adolph I'd return as soon as possible and took a few weeks off to go back east by stage and train. I wrote Mary I was coming and . . . well, to cut this story short, we were married and went on a two-week trip to Bermuda for a honeymoon. It was wonderful having money to spend."

He paused to take another long draw at his beer. "Talking is thirsty work." He set the mug aside. "Now, where was I? Oh, yes, we returned and planned to go by ship around Cape Horn and settle in San Francisco so as to be nearer the mine operation that had grown considerably. Aboard ship I came down with a fever and was confined to our cabin. It took us weeks to double the horn and we began to run short of food. We finally made it around, but we were out of supplies and the captain had to put in at Valparaiso, Chile. I was carried ashore because they were afraid I'd die without medical attention. My wife found a doctor there who finally brought me around. While I recovered my strength, we had to wait two weeks in a rented room before we could find a berth on a steamer heading north to California. By this time I'd been gone for more than six months with only two letters exchanged between me and Adolph. In his second letter, he thanked me for selling out to him, and wished me well. At first I was puzzled because there were no plans for me to sell. I began to suspect something, but then I got too sick to respond. A later telegraph message of mine went unanswered."

He took a deep breath and sighed, his eyes going blank as if staring at some inner scene. For a few moments, Charvein saw, not a bandit chief, but a human being with a severely wounded spirit.

"When I finally tracked down Adolph, he handed me a notice that our partnership was dissolved and a document, allegedly signed by me, that sold him my half of the mine for $20,000. The signature had been forged on the bill of sale that was back-dated to the week before I left California. And I had been paid nothing. I sued him. When it came to court, I lost, based on the phony evidence presented. After paying my attorney and the court costs, I had nothing left. I had to telegraph Mary's parents to send money for her passage back to Carolina so she could live with them for whatever time it would take me to get back on my feet."

He paused and gingerly put his fingers to his swollen nose.

"During the legal proceedings, four men contacted me who had a grudge against Grindell for one reason or another—mostly for being cheated of their wages. Three of the men were from Ireland. The five of us decided we couldn't let this travesty go unchallenged, so we formed a group to balance the scales. By this time, Grindell had moved fast and opened a jewelry store in Los Angeles. He even had artisans crafting gold trinkets for him. For a share of the profits my new friends and I recruited four more men who were in key jobs, such as a Western Union telegrapher and train dispatcher at Los Angeles to keep us informed of the schedule of Grindell's jewelry shipments. And the rest you know."

"How does that hurt Grindell?" Charvein asked. "Wells Fargo has a policy of reimbursing shippers for any losses. He's not out anything."

"I admit it has probably been only an aggravation to him because his shipments of ornate jewelry have been stolen, and his customers probably lost."

"So you *did* melt down the jewelry, mint the coins, and started giving them out to the poor peasants?" Charvein asked.

"Yes." He smiled. "It was just a classic case of playing Robin Hood. We unburdened this particular rich thief and redistributed the altered gold to those who really needed it. Of course, we had to save some for expenses—wages and food for my men and reimbursement to me for being swindled." He smiled faintly. "And in the process the newspapers have made the Border Brigands rather famous."

"Notorious would be a better description."

"Well, have it your way. I'm something of a romantic, as you may have gathered. The name has a certain flair, don't you think? 'James Gordon Flynn and his Merry Men' just doesn't have the same ring." He chuckled.

"And all that other stuff, like the caped, masked rider distributing gold coins at midnight?"

"Just drama and play-acting—to give our operation some class. As long as we were in this for retribution, I decided we might as well have some fun at the same time—mysterious highwaymen balancing the scales of justice."

"So I guessed right," Charvein said. "Sandoval suspected there was a lot more behind all this, but I never knew until now it was a personal grudge."

"You'll notice that we never killed anyone while we disrupted your shipments."

"Yes. But just by chance nobody died when your man threw dynamite into the express car. And one of my assistants was later shot in the leg."

"Sometimes it's impossible to restrain impetuous young men in the heat of conflict. It would not have happened had I been there in person."

"Murder is a hanging offense. You had someone try to ambush us at Gila Bend."

"That was done without my knowledge or consent. My men were only trying to protect me and our operation."

"Then you don't have them under control."

"Perhaps. I can't be responsible for what they do on their own. In any case, I'm not afraid of human law. But killing is against the law of God."

"So you drew the line at killing. 'Thou Shalt Not Kill' is observed, but anything else is all right? Another commandment says, 'Thou Shalt Not Steal.' "

"It's nice to match wits with a man of intelligence," Flynn smiled. "Even if you did break my nose." He dabbed at his face with the wet towel. "I'm trying to tell you, this was not stealing. I'm just taking back what is rightfully mine."

Charvein took a swallow of his warm beer. If this eccentric man didn't believe in killing, maybe it was safe to get a bit bolder. "As long as you seem to be drawing moral and ethical lines here," he countered, "what about Christ's admonition to turn the other cheek? I'm no Biblical scholar by any means, but didn't He say something to the effect that if a man goes to court over your coat, you should give him your shirt as well?"

"There was also some teaching that if your brother is in the wrong you should try to correct him, more than once, and get your friends to try. But if he doesn't listen to you, turn him over to the authorities."

"But not to take the law into your own hands."

"I took Grindell to court, but because of his false evidence, there was a miscarriage of justice."

There's no reasoning with this man, Charvein thought. *He's justified his actions to his own satisfaction.* He tried again. "What about, 'Vengeance is mine. I will repay,' saith the Lord?"

"This is not about vengeance; this is about justice. As the Lord's Prayer says, 'Thy will be done, on earth as it is in heaven.' Are we not God's instruments on this earth? Why else do we have laws, judges, and railroad detectives like yourself?"

A heavy, dark-skinned man with a grizzled beard appeared in the open doorway. Charvein had not seen him before.

"It's going on midnight," he said.

Flynn nodded. "Get underway."

Charvein felt a twinge in his stomach. What would happen to him now? Would Flynn actually spare his life on moral principles? The handsome leader of the Border Brigands had admitted his gang had pulled the armed robberies of the trains, wounding at least two, stolen thousands of dollars' worth of gold jewelry, attempted to shoot him and Sandoval from ambush, and had wounded Sandoval when he'd sneaked into their hideout.

Flynn couldn't very well just turn Charvein loose with that kind of knowledge. Or could he? "Face" apparently didn't know Sandoval had snatched a piece of jewelry as evidence. But if it ever came to court, Flynn could deny any knowledge of where the necklace had come from. The gang leader would have to be apprehended with the jewelry in his possession and have the eyewitness testimony of Charvein, Sandoval, and Lucy Barkley before a conviction might be possible.

Yet all that was moot if Flynn was never caught, arrested, and tried. And right now that seemed a remote possibility.

Flynn rose from his chair and stretched. He finished his beer, then shoved the Webley under his belt. Picking up the Winchester carbine from the table, he said, "As soon as we have steam up, we'll be off. You'll be our guest for a time."

Charvein started to question him further, but held off. He'd find out his fate soon enough, and almost didn't want to know.

Flynn ushered him at gunpoint into the moonlight outside and forward along the main deck. They crossed a secured cargo hatch, and Flynn stopped at another watertight door. "You'll share the hold with our gear for now," he said. "Even though there're air vents, it'll probably be a mite stuffy down there. Nothing to worry about, though. You won't be with us long."

Charvein's stomach knotted. The door swung outward. Flynn gave him a shove and he stumbled down two steps into the blackness. The door banged shut behind him.

CHAPTER 28

Charvein stood still, breathing heavily in the darkness. It was his imagination, but the blackness was almost smothering. There was plenty of fresh air.

He felt around and discovered he was on a landing. Finding a handrail, he guided himself down three more steps to what seemed the bottom of the hold. Rough, wooden planks were under his boots.

Trying mightily to get a grip on his nerves, he struggled to ignore the realization of where he was. What was in Flynn's mind? What did he mean by the offhand remark that Charvein would not be with them long? Only one thing. In spite of the outlaw's avowed disbelief in killing, he was going to murder Charvein, and maybe dump him overboard, once they were well south in the gulf.

Given Flynn's convoluted reasoning, he would somehow justify it as ridding the world of an evil Wells Fargo lawman who was interfering with Flynn's making the world a fairer, more equitable place. He knew it would not be difficult for Flynn to rationalize murder in some such manner.

His knees were feeling a bit shaky, so he sat down where he was, and took a deep breath, wondering how long before he met his fate. Was there anything he could do to prevent it, or even to escape? Besides Logan, the man whose finger he'd shot off in the struggle, Charvein had seen three others besides Flynn—the two who had subdued him, and the grizzled man he assumed was the captain or helmsman.

There were very likely three or four others aboard, either Flynn's own men or members of a crew it would take to run this boat. In any case, unarmed and locked in the hold, he was also outnumbered at least five or six to one.

A short time later, with steam up, the boat trembled and a rhythmic throb began. The paddlewheel was turning and they were underway.

A boat like this would be expensive to buy or build. If Charvein had been in Flynn's place, he would have leased the boat with crew. It would have been much cheaper—all paid for with Grindell's money.

Did Grindell know he had a mortal enemy who was behind the robbery of his gold jewelry? Had he even speculated about it, or had he left all that to Wells Fargo? Maybe the swindler was too busy getting richer and chasing women. Flynn would certainly have let Grindell know that his former partner was taking revenge. Otherwise, where would be the satisfaction? The recompense in gold was one thing, but Flynn would want his old enemy to know his ex-partner was exacting vengeance as well as repayment.

As long as Flynn was in a talkative mood, Charvein wished he'd questioned him further about his operation. Was Face closing up shop before they were caught? Or was he just moving somewhere deeper into Mexico to start up again at another location? If that were the case, how could his gunmen rob trains across the border and still ride so far south to their new hideout? It would take several days, making the journey with the stolen loot even more hazardous. Except for the danger of open fires on a seagoing vessel, they might even do their gold melting and hand minting aboard this boat. Charvein guessed that the molds and dies and other equipment needed was all here in the hold with him, but he wasn't about to stumble around in the dark to find out and risk hurting himself. His side still had a dull ache where he'd fallen on the rifle stock. He wanted to conserve his energy for an escape attempt. He'd eaten before leaving the hotel and this, along with the beer he'd drunk in the cabin above, had renewed his strength from the long ride. But it was now past midnight and he was beginning to feel drowsy. The gentle motion of the boat and the dim swishing sound of water moving alongside the hull increased the feeling.

He stretched out on the hard planks, put his arm under his head, and dozed off.

Some time later he was jarred awake by the banging of the door. A hurricane lantern flashed its light down the stairs.

He sat up, stiffly, squinting at the sudden brightness.

"Time to go."

Charvein yawned, and stretched his arms and shoulders. Then, taking his time, he bent over to stretch his legs and back. Whatever was going to happen in the next few minutes, he wanted to be physically ready.

Pretending to be stiff, tired, and disoriented, he shuffled across the gently heaving deck to the stairs. Inside, he was alert and coiled like a spring.

Flynn was waiting at the top, and stepped back for Charvein to pass through the door, still shining the light in his face. Charvein felt a pistol muzzle press against his ribs.

Charvein inhaled deeply of the fresh salt air, felt the cool breeze, and heard the steady swishing of the paddlewheel. The boat was not slowing down for any port. He sensed no other men were close by. It was just him and Flynn. He paused.

"I regret you can't finish this trip with us," Flynn said, still hidden behind the partially shuttered storm lantern. "I would enjoy the conversation of an educated man all the way to Los Angeles."

"I could come along." Charvein stalled for time to let his eyes adjust to the light that was reflecting off a nearby bulkhead. "I don't eat much."

Flynn laughed. "And a sense of humor, too. I'm still irritated about you breaking my nose, but I brought that on myself. I don't hold grudges."

It was Charvein's turn to snort a derisive laugh. "You don't hold grudges? Then I suppose you and Grindell are best friends."

"I have a rendezvous with Mister Adolphus Grindell." Flynn's voice was suddenly cold and hard. "You were right that taking a few of his shipments was only a temporary setback—a minor inconvenience. I hope Adolph is enjoying my portion of that gold mine because he won't be spending it much longer." He shoved the gun into Charvein's side. "Move that way."

"You don't want me to come along as a witness?" Charvein shuffled toward the starboard rail, desperately trying to keep him talking. Prideful men like Flynn loved to brag about themselves and their enterprises. "I could give your side of the story when you're arrested."

"You have a knack of interfering in other people's affairs," Flynn grated. "There will be no witnesses and there will be no arrests. It's between me and that damned lying thief. I've been planning this for a long time. It will be the final act of the play where justice triumphs—a great moment of satisfaction."

"But you . . ."

Charvein wasn't expecting the hard shove that sent him headfirst over the waist-high rail. He hit the water and went under, instinctively holding his breath. A gurgling noise replaced all sound for several seconds until he popped to the surface, gasping. The dim bulk of the steamer was rapidly churning away.

Flynn flashed the lantern beam toward him, and then beyond. "The shore is only a hundred yards that way!" he yelled. Then the lantern was shuttered.

Charvein continued to tread water, numbly staring at the dim whiteness where the stern wheel was beating the sea water to foam.

I should have jumped him when I had the chance, he thought. But he realized he would've gotten a bullet for his trouble. Even if he'd somehow managed to overpower Flynn, the other men on the boat would probably have killed him.

Hoping the outlaw leader had told the truth about the nearness of the shore, Charvein turned and struck out in a sidestroke. After a few minutes he looked up but could see no sign of land in the utter blackness. His boots were filled with water and felt like weights on his feet, dragging at him. A small wave slopped saltwater into his mouth and he coughed. *Maybe you don't believe in murder, but you've killed me,* he thought, beginning to panic.

He rested for a few seconds, then rolled over onto his back and tried to relax while he kicked and paddled.

A partial moon broke free of clouds and he turned again and looked ahead. There! A shoreline only about forty yards away. With renewed energy and hope he kicked toward it. Several minutes later, his boots touched bottom and he staggered up, streaming water. He lay facedown on the warm rocks until he'd recovered his breath, then turned and sat up.

He pulled off his boots and poured the water out.

Across the gulf to the east, a streak of dim light painted the horizon. Dawn was coming up. He'd slept in the hold longer than he realized.

But with the coming of the sun would come heat and thirst. He had no water, no hat, no knife, gun, or map. Nor did he have any idea where he was, except somewhere on the Baja Peninsula.

CHAPTER 29

Even though the air was anything but cold, he shivered in his wet clothes. He wrung out his socks and then stripped off the rest of his clothes and did the same. Being naked, he felt warmer without the clinging wet cotton against his skin. He sat on a flat stone, facing east, and watched the day coming.

Everything was silent and still, with no breeze. Even the surface of the gulf was nearly flat with only slight ripples. As the sun cleared the distant low mountains, it seemed to rise quicker, and soon he felt its rays beginning to heat up the desert. His skin was warm and dry now and he recoiled at the clammy feeling, but pulled his clothes back on and struggled into the wet boots. The clothes would dry on him quickly in the desert air.

He seemed to have landed on a long curved beach of some kind that was composed more of fine, alluvial dirt than sand. He got up and walked up over a hill about 30 feet high to see what lay beyond him to the west. Desert. In the distance he thought he could make out a strip of blue. The sea? Or a mirage? He hoped it was a mirage or he was probably on an island. No sign of human habitation anywhere. Low desert mountains rose to the right and left of him, apparently several miles away, although it was difficult to judge distance in the clear air. No trees or shrubbery that would indicate any water. He came back down to the beach and began hunting for something to make a hat out of. Without a knife, he couldn't cut any of the desert plants. Maybe there were some reeds or palm fronds washed up he could use.

Some two hours later, he was baking in the sun. Stripping off his now-dry clothes, he dropped them on the beach and waded back into the ocean. The bottom dropped off fairly rapidly and he let himself sink down under the water to wet his head and cool off. With the heating of midday, a breeze sprang up, and he was comfortable as long as he stayed submerged up to his neck, although he had to turn away from the glare on the water.

Twice he came out onto the beach but almost immediately realized the sun was beginning to burn his white skin. The hot breeze and the sun dried him off so quickly the grainy crystals of salt on his body felt like sand. He went back in, and stayed until his skin was wrinkled.

He had no feeling of panic—only hopelessness. He was in a fix and would likely die of thirst and exposure here. He could absorb some water through his skin by osmosis, but not nearly enough. The Mexican villages were few and widely spaced. Without water and food he could not walk a hundred miles or more to some settlement—even if he knew which direction to go. Flynn had to know he was giving Charvein a death sentence when he shoved him overboard. How would he rationalize this killing? Flynn might have started out with good intentions to redress a wrong, but the hatred had come to possess him.

Charvein bobbed along in the water, his feet barely touching bottom when a flash of white caught his eye. It was a seagull, then another. There were a dozen or more. He watched them wheel and dive. Suddenly he saw what had attracted them. They were following a southbound fishing boat a quarter mile away. The big, gaff-rigged sail was drawing the boat along on the port tack and seemed to be moving slowly in the morning breeze.

Charvein's heart leapt and he struggled out of the water, waving and shouting and jumping up and down.

But the boat continued on its way.

He looked frantically for something to signal with. Fifty feet away, he found a broken bottle and snatched up the largest piece of glass.

Holding it to catch the morning sun, he wiggled it until he could see where the reflected ray was touching the sail. He worked it down until he was flashing the spot of light on a figure beneath the boom inside the boat.

For a long minute there was nothing. Was the man facing the other way? Squinting, Charvein focused every ounce of his concentration on pinpointing the lancing reflection.

Finally, the big sail jibed over in the light breeze and the boat swung toward him.

He waved and jumped up and down to be sure the fisherman could see his white naked body in the bright sun.

"Thank God!" he panted. "Thank God!"

He reached for his clothes and began to dress.

Charvein finished gulping his fourth cup of water, dribbling it down his shirt in his haste. He wiped his mouth with the back of his hand. *"Muchas gracias!"* he gasped, exhausting about half his knowledge of Spanish.

"De nada," the lean man replied, eyeing him from his seat at the tiller.

"Where are we?" Charvein asked. "Where are you going?" He looked from the helmsman to his passenger.

"No habla Ingles," the man at the tiller replied with a shrug. From beneath the brim of a straw hat, his eyes were only slits in the dark, on a seamed face, as if from years of squinting into the sun's reflection on the sea. The fisherman could have been anywhere from forty to sixty years old.

"I can answer that," the only other occupant of the boat replied with no trace of an accent. He was a big, bluff man with a short, gray-streaked brown beard. "Name's Jerrold Conway," he said, thrusting out a hand.

"Marc Charvein," he replied, gripping the calloused palm. "You an American?"

"Right. I'm a mine foreman from Nogales. Come down three or four times a year to fish. Miguel, here, is the best fishing boat captain in Guaymas." He turned to the man at the tiller and said something in Spanish. Miguel smiled and nodded.

"You're damned lucky you got our attention," Conway continued. "No water on that uninhabited island. It's called Angel de la Guardia—the second largest island in the gulf."

"Guardian Angel?"

"Yeah. Most people just call it Archangel Island. But I reckon it was your guardian angel today." He gestured at the fishing rods stowed along the bulwark. "We caught only a few small ones overnight—water too warm, I reckon. Anyway, we gave it up at daylight and were heading back to Guaymas when we saw your signal. How'd you come to be out there alone with no food or water, or even a hat?"

"Well, it's a long story. I'm a Wells Fargo detective," he said, pulling out his damp billfold and showing his badge. "Had a run-in with some men I'm after. I got the worst of it and they marooned me there last night."

"Really? Where are they now?"

"Who knows? Their steamer was headed south. Bound for California."

Conway nodded. "Pretty good distance. Close to fifteen hundred miles, I'd guess. But, if they don't stop, they could make Los Angeles in a week or less."

A freshening breeze heeled the boat slightly, and Conway sat down next to the port rail, bracing his sandaled foot against the hatch coaming. "Where you going from here?"

"I need to get back to the states as quick as possible, and see if I can head them off."

"Well, there's a train runs from Guaymas straight north through Hermosillo to Nogales," he said. "It's about two-hundred forty miles. Mexican railroads sometimes aren't too reliable, but this one's only six years old and it runs on time, mostly. That'll get you across the line, but not close to California."

"That's good news. After I get to Nogales I can make it from there."

"You could take a stage from Nogales to Tucson and then catch the Southern Pacific to the coast."

Charvein nodded. "I know. I work on that train."

"The slow part will be the stage to Tucson. We have to ship our ore by freight wagon to the railroad."

"What's one-way fare to Nogales?"

"Twenty dollars."

Charvein groaned. He had only two remaining silver dollars and one sawbuck. "I'll have to hop a freight."

"I wouldn't advise that," Conway said. "If the bulls catch you, you could be spending time in the calaboose. And, believe me, you don't want to see the inside of a Mexican jail. Cockroaches and scorpions have been breeding in most of them since the time of Juarez. If you have no money for a fine or bribe, they'll likely forget you're even in there."

"I need to offer something to Miguel for rescuing me," Charvein said.

"No need. I always give him a generous tip, and I'll tell him this one was from you."

"I'm grateful."

"As a matter of fact, I can lend you the fare to Nogales. That way you can save your money for food or stage fare to Tucson."

Relief washed over Charvein. His luck was, indeed, beginning to change. "I'll get your address and reimburse you."

"That's okay. It's not that much. Glad to help out a fellow American. I have a good salary and no family to support. If I decide I want it back," he added with a grin, "I can always bill Wells Fargo."

Charvein turned to look south. "How far to Guaymas?"

"Oh, you can relax. We won't get there until at least noon tomorrow. We'll sleep aboard, and take turns steering and standing watch." He glanced at the sky, then said something to Miguel who replied in rapid Spanish. "He says it will be a clear, moonlit night, so we won't have to anchor come dark."

CHAPTER 30

Late the next afternoon, after they'd gone ashore, Charvein insisted on treating Conway to supper.

"The passenger train leaves out about ten tonight." The foreman cut off a piece of fried fish. "Arrives at Nogales at eight in the morning. I ride that train a good bit and know the schedule by heart."

Charvein was allaying his hunger and eating as much as he could hold. No telling when he'd eat again.

Conway, making conversation, pumped him about the nature of the case he was working on, but Charvein gave only vague answers, telling him he couldn't discuss the details until the case was resolved.

"One way or the other, it'll be in the papers—at least in Tucson," he assured Conway, when they finished. Charvein handed the waiter his last two silver dollars, keeping his American $5 greenback.

"It's been a pleasure," Conway said. "More rewarding than any fishing trip I've been on lately." He slipped a double eagle into Charvein's hand and pointed the way to the depot.

Charvein thanked him and walked the several blocks to the adobe railroad station. After buying a one-way ticket to Nogales, he sat down on a bench in the waiting room, and picked up a discarded newspaper to kill the time.

He found himself staring blankly at the print he couldn't read while his mind wandered. What had become of Lucy,

Sandoval, and Diego? Were they safe? Had they made it to the border?

By the time the train reaches Nogales in the morning, it will be more than two days since I was marooned, he thought. Conway estimated a week by steamer to Los Angeles. *If he was right, that means I have only five days more to reach LA and warn Grindell.* Maybe he didn't need to travel that far. If he could get to Yuma and arrest telegrapher Dennis Dugan, someone else could wire Grindell a warning. But the message would never be delivered if the Los Angeles telegrapher was another of Flynn's informants who were paid to keep him apprised of Grindell's shipments.

Charvein got up and paced restlessly around the waiting room. He felt stymied. He would never reach Grindell in time. It was difficult to feel any sympathy for Adolph Grindell, whom Charvein had never met, after the story Flynn had told about the man, and Lucy's experience with him. But Charvein would not be doing his duty if he didn't at least try to warn the wealthy mine owner that his former partner was on his way to possibly murder him. What would happen when they met? Flynn had seemed firm in his opposition to killing, yet he'd thrown Charvein off the steamer to almost certain death. And that was only for interference with his plans. What more would he do to a man he'd hated for a long time? Charvein felt certain Flynn would find a way to kill the man, no matter how he had to justify it.

Charvein noticed several other passengers in the waiting room glancing furtively at him. He realized he must look like a panhandling tramp. He was sunburned, hadn't shaved for days, his hair had been combed only with his fingers, and he'd been sleeping in his clothes, which were stained with salt streaks. Except for bathing in the ocean, he hadn't been able to clean up since he'd washed in a creek several days before. He went back and sat down, trying to remain inconspicuous. The long

June twilight settled in, and he noticed the big wall clock indicated it was only a half-hour until train time.

The train jolted to a stop in a squeal of brakes near eight the next morning. Charvein looked out at the border town of Nogales tucked into the folds of the green hills.

He stepped into the aisle and stretched. In spite of the hard seats in the day coach, he'd leaned against the window and dozed off as soon as the train pulled out at 10:10 the night before. He was exhausted from having slept the previous night on the deck of a fishing sloop and the night before that on the hard planks in the hold of the steamer. Compared to those beds, the wicker seats of the train felt like a feather tick. He'd partially awakened when the train stopped at Hermosillo, but had quickly gone back to sleep.

He shuffled to the end of the car in line with other detraining passengers. Stepping down onto the depot platform, he knew he was still in Mexico and had to get across to the other side without being seen. Except for his Wells Fargo badge pinned inside his billfold, he had nothing to identify himself. Money greased the skids with border guards, but his only means of a bribe was the $5 bill he carried, and that was hardly enough. Besides, he'd need that before he got home. He couldn't waste time haggling with either American or Mexican officials, enduring hours of questioning and possibly being put into a cell while his story was being checked out. His goal was the stage depot on the American side.

He'd never been to Nogales, but sauntered out of town, carefully watching others on the street. No one gave a second glance to a dirty, scruffy, unarmed man who looked as if he were looking for a handout. Sometimes it was good to be invisible.

Three miles beyond the last buildings, he found himself in a rugged canyon between two hills, choked with cholla, prickly pear, and thick stands of mesquite. He saw tracks of small animals, but no hoofprints, boot marks, or any indication humans had been here recently. He had no idea where the border actually was, but he concealed himself for twenty minutes in the shade of a thick stand of mesquite, watching and listening. The desert hills were silent. No sounds reached him. In case armed guards were posted along the border, he patiently waited another half-hour before he moved.

Two blasts of a locomotive steam whistle in the distance announced the train was starting its return trip south. He stepped out and began to weave his way past "jumping cholla," plowing up the soft, alluvial sand into the cleft between the hills.

It took him until early afternoon to work his way into what had to be the Arizona Territory. Sliding unnoticed into Nogales, he saw signs on stores in English and knew he was on the American side of the town that straddled the border.

A loafer on the porch of a saloon directed him to the stage station and he walked there, hot, dirty, and thirsty, praying he had enough for the fare to Tucson. He did, with three dollars to spare. And the stage would be loading for Tucson in ten minutes. His luck was holding. Maybe he could beat Flynn to Los Angeles after all.

The stagecoach was delayed reaching Tucson when a rear wheel fell into a deep rut and broke a spoke. The driver and guard had done some makeshift repairs, but the team had proceeded at a walk until they reached Tucson sometime in the early morning hours.

Charvein, nearly dead on his feet, fumbled his way to the Southern Pacific depot and dozed the rest of the night on a bench in the waiting room.

He woke up at dawn, stiff and sore, realizing more than three full days had been used up since he'd parted company with

Flynn—probably half the estimated time he'd allowed himself to reach Los Angeles.

The Wells Fargo office was located in the depot and Charvein was waiting when they opened at seven in the morning. He presented his badge to a man he didn't know.

"I'm undercover," he explained when the man with the sleeve garters and the waxed mustache regarded him dubiously. "I've been in Mexico and I'm on the trail of some robbers. I must be on the next westbound passenger express."

"It's coming out of San Antone," the man said. "Not due in here until noon tomorrow."

"Nothing sooner?"

The man shook his head. "Of course, there's a local westbound leaving at 10:15 this morning. Mixed freight. Makes all the stops. Unless you want a long, rough ride, I'd advise you to wait for the express."

"I'll take the freight," Charvein said, not wanting to kill another day and a half, waiting. "When the express catches us on a siding, I'll flag it down."

The Wells Fargo man shook his head. "Might want to talk to the dispatcher about that. The express will be highballed through and probably won't stop except for an emergency."

Charvein sought out the Tucson dispatcher and discovered there was little chance of halting the express, even for official business. "She'll make a brief mail stop at Gila Bend," he said, "but, except for water stops, that's it until Yuma."

Charvein studied the enlarged route map on the wall. "Gila Bend is just over a hundred miles. I'll have a twenty-six-hour head start. Should make it easily. I'll intercept it there." He went out to find something to eat and to slake his thirst.

Charvein flashed his Wells Fargo badge as a pass to board the California Flyer in Gila Bend the next night at 9:30. The uniformed conductor nodded and then looked at Charvein. "Lemme see that." He reached for the badge and examined it closer. "I'm on a case," Charvein explained, realizing how he must look, "and really in a hurry." It was nearly five days now since Flynn had dumped him, and he was only at Gila Bend. He was also completely broke and exhausted after a jolting, interminable twenty-hour ride on the freight. His last three dollars had gone for food the day before.

He went aboard the coach and found a seat away from the other passengers and slumped down wearily on the velvet cushions. A few minutes later, the train began to roll, and in another few minutes, he was asleep.

"I've already heard the story from Sandoval and the woman," Barton Coughlin, the Wells Fargo superintendent interrupted when Charvein began to blurt out a brief version of his chase the next afternoon in Yuma.

"So they made it! Thank God!"

"Yeah. Sandoval is resting at a hotel. Doc Vance was in town and treated him. I don't know where the woman is at the moment."

"Her name is Lucy Barkley."

"Yeah, that's it—Lucy. There was a Mexican boy with . . ."

"Yes, yes. They're here and all right?"

"Yes."

"Here's the part of the story they don't know . . ." Charvein went on to tell his end of the tale, leaving out most of the detail. "I have to get to Los Angeles and warn Aldolph Grindell. Flynn will catch up with him in less than twenty-four hours."

"I'll wire the police."

"Won't do any good. Flynn has a Western Union spy on that end."

Coughlin looked at him, thoughtfully. "Based on what

Sandoval and Lucy told me, I had the local telegrapher, Dennis Dugan, arrested and charged with conspiracy to commit murder and armed robbery."

"Good, but that won't help me get to Los Angeles any faster."

"You're in no condition to go. You're dead on your feet." He reached inside his coat, brought out a leather wallet, and handed Charvein three twenty-dollar bills. "You have just enough time to get cleaned up before the westbound Flyer pulls out. Take a Pullman overnight to the coast. Commandeer a berth if you have to." He paused, then opened his desk drawer, and retrieved a short-barreled Colt. "Take this, and I hope to God you don't need it."

CHAPTER 31

The slowing train awoke Charvein from a dreamless sleep. Coming back from a long way off, it took him a few seconds to recall where he was.

Then he remembered.

He sat up in his berth, feeling more rested than he had in weeks, and reached for the clean shirt and pants hanging on a nearby hook. Bathed, shaved, with money and a weapon in his pockets, he felt recovered enough to take on nearly anything.

Rubbing sleep from his eyes, he pulled aside the curtain and saw the pastel-colored Los Angeles depot sliding into view.

He had to hurry. His flat stomach was making angry noises, but breakfast could wait.

By the time the train ground to a halt, he was at the end of the car waiting for the porter to open the door. He dashed out into the fresh early morning, dodged among the baggage carts and waiting passengers, and hailed one of the hacks lined up under the date palms in the street out front. He leapt into the back of the open carriage.

"Where to?"

"Grindell's Jewelers."

The burly Negro driver twisted around to look at Charvein. "You mean that factory that makes all the jewelry?"

"Yeah, yeah, that's it. Hurry!"

"Ain't no need to rush."

"What?"

The driver picked up a copy of the *Los Angeles Daily Times* lying on the seat beside him and handed it back.

A headline read, JEWELRY EMPORIUM BURNED. Beneath, in smaller type was: *Owner Shot in Daring Daylight Robbery*

Torched Grindell Factory A Total Loss

Charvein scanned the rest of the article and saw that Adolph Grindell was still alive. *"Doctors confident they can save mine owner's legs, but bullets to both knees will likely leave him crippled for life."*

Charvein blew out his breath in a long sigh. He was too late. Flynn had evened the score with his cheating partner.

He glanced back at the piece and read the robbers had escaped, carting off several sacks of jewelry. Various eyewitnesses didn't agree on the number of robbers—some said three, some four. But two store employees had heard Grindell and one of the black-haired robbers shouting vile names at each other before shots were fired. The coal oil chandeliers were smashed and the wooden building was ablaze in seconds.

Police had questioned Grindell at the hospital, but he refused to state whether or not he knew his assailant. The robbers had scattered in several different directions, and police were searching the city, watching the rail depots and the waterfront. *Police confident of an early arrest in the case.*

"Yeah, I'll bet," Charvein murmured. He looked up at the white-shirted driver. "Take me there anyway."

An hour later, Charvein was viewing a pile of smoldering ruins. One pumper was still on the scene, spraying water on hot spots. The street in front of the former factory was littered with splintered wood and shards of broken glass. Several dozen spectators were milling outside the wooden sawhorses that blockaded the street. A uniformed policeman patrolled the

227

scene. Flynn had made a thorough job of it, and he'd beaten Charvein by about fifteen hours.

He turned away toward the waiting hack. He'd wire Coughlin with a report and ask if his boss wanted him to report first to the Los Angeles police before returning. He'd also offer to work the express car on his return trip to Yuma.

Six days later, Charvein sat at a table in the Harvey House in the Yuma depot with Lucy Barkley, Carlos Sandoval, and Diego Sanchez. They'd just finished a late breakfast and were sipping coffee in the nearly empty restaurant.

"According to a wire Coughlin got from the LA police, Flynn and his men are still on the run," Sandoval said. Though still sore and tightly bandaged, his side was healing well. And he'd even reached the point where he felt comfortable removing the brace from his broken arm.

"A well-planned operation," Charvein said. "Three employees up front agreed that five men hit the place fast, each filled a sack with gold and jewelry, two others torched the building, and they lit out. In the few minutes this took, Flynn dealt with Grindell.

"Flynn must've anchored somewhere away from the harbor because there was no sign of the steamer. And the railroad depot was being watched. At least I was able to give a description of Flynn and a couple of the others who might've been there, so the police and the Pinkertons will have something to go on."

"They're probably out of the country by now," Sandoval said. "If it had been me, I would have come ashore at some deserted beach south of LA."

"Would have been hard for each man carrying a sack of loot to disappear in the city in daylight," Lucy said. "I was lugging a heavy cross of gold in a leather bag last year, and I could not have gotten very far with that if someone was chasing me. At least Wells Fargo won't have to worry about any more robberies from the Border Brigands," she added, brightly.

"Yeah. Like the James gang and all the rest, their time is over," Charvein agreed. "Now that Flynn has gotten his revenge, that will be it for him. He didn't strike me as a hardened criminal. From now on, I'd guess he'll have a bigger fight with his conscience than with the law."

"You think he'll go back to his wife, Mary?" Lucy asked. "If the police can find out her maiden name, they might be lying in wait for Flynn at her parents' place in Carolina."

Charvein shrugged. "I told the law all I knew, and Flynn never mentioned his wife's maiden name."

They fell silent for a minute, all with their own thoughts.

"Did I tell you Coughlin is going to take the cost of my rented horse and saddle out of my wages?" Charvein said.

"Really? That's pretty cheap after what you did for the company," Sandoval said.

"Charging me for the lost Wells Fargo Winchester, too."

Sandoval shook his head. "I'll give Coughlin that new rifle of Canto's to make up for it. If anybody asks, I found it in Mexico." He grinned. "If you left that rented horse at the Puerto Peñasco livery, why don't we go down there and claim him?" he suggested.

"You're not in any shape for a trip like that, and I have no inclination to go back," Charvein said with conviction. "Besides, you won't be able to get away. Once you're healed up, you'll be working full-time for Wells Fargo."

"What about you, Diego?" Sandoval asked, turning to the teen. "What are your plans?"

"I do not know." The boy shook his head, solemnly. "I will not return to Mexico. I hope to find a job here or hide out if the law comes to take me back."

"After I told Coughlin what you did for us, I doubt you'll be deported," Sandoval said. "Maybe you can ask for asylum."

"I have a better idea," Charvein said.

All eyes turned to him.

"Since you're an orphan, Lucy and I can adopt you."

Lucy's eyes widened and her mouth fell open. "We? . . . adopt?" she stammered.

Charvein got up, moved to her chair, leaned down, and kissed her. "What do you say?"

"That sounds like some kind of cross-grained proposal. I think you've been out in the sun too long."

"No I haven't. Will you marry me?" She stood up and hugged his neck for several long seconds. When she backed away, she wore a dazzling smile. "Yes. And the first person I want to invite to the wedding is Frances Cain, my old friend at the LA Harvey House."

"And there's a mine supervisor in Nogales named Jerrold Conway I want to add to the list," Charvein said.

Sandoval and Diego looked at each other, then lifted their coffee cups in a silent toast.

ABOUT THE AUTHOR

Tim Champlin was born John Michael Champlin in Fargo, North Dakota, the son of a large-animal veterinarian and a school teacher.

He grew up in Nebraska, Missouri, and Arizona, where he was graduated from St. Mary's High School, Phoenix, before moving to Tennessee.

After earning a BS degree in English from Middle Tennessee State College, he declined an offer to become a Border Patrol Agent with the U.S. Immigration Service in order to finish work on a Master of Arts degree in English from Peabody College (now part of Vanderbilt University).

After 39 rejection slips, he sold his first piece of writing in 1971 to *Boating* magazine. The photo article, "Sailing the Mississippi," is a dramatic account of a 3-day, 75-mile solo adventure on the big river from Memphis to Helena, Arkansas, in a 16-foot fiberglass sailboat built from a kit in his basement. His only means of propulsion were current, sails, and a canoe paddle.

Since then, 36 of his historical novels have been published. Most are set in the frontier West. A handful touch on the Civil War. Other books deal with juvenile time travel, a clash between Jack the Ripper and Annie Oakley, the lost Templar treasure, and Mark Twain's hidden recordings.

Besides books, he's written several dozen short stories and nonfiction articles, plus 2 children's books.

Twice he has been runner-up for a Spur Award from Western Writers of America—once for a novel (*The Secret of Lodestar*) and once for a short story ("Color at Forty-Mile").

Tim is still creating enthralling new tales. Most of his books are available online as ebooks.

In 1994 he retired after 30 years of work in the U.S. Civil Service. He and his wife, Ellen, have 3 grown children and 10 grandchildren. Active in sports all his life, his hobbies still include biking, shooting, sailing, and tennis.